BELIEVE ME

BELIEVE ME
PATRICIA PEARSON

VINTAGE CANADA

VINTAGE CANADA EDITION, 2006

Published in Canada by Vintage Canada, a division of Random House of Canada
Limited, Toronto, in 2006. Originally published in hardcover in Canada by
Random House Canada, a division of Random House of Canada Limited, Toronto,
in 2005. Distributed by Random House of Canada Limited, Toronto.

Vintage Canada and colophon are registered trademarks of
Random House of Canada Limited.

www.randomhouse.ca

LIBRARY AND ARCHIVES CANADA CATALOGUING IN PUBLICATION

Pearson, Patricia, 1964–
Believe me / Patricia Pearson.

ISBN-13: 978-0-679-31346-5
ISBN-10: 0-679-31346-X

I. Title.

PS8581.E3884B44 2006   C813'.6   C2005-905098-5

Printed and bound in Canada

2 4 6 8 9 7 5 3 1

For Clara and Geoffrey
The loves of my life

1

Lately, I've been thinking about death.

Actually, I haven't.

I don't like to think about death. Whenever the subject of death springs to mind, the two thoughts that form in my brain are *scary*, and *go away*. It's my son, Lester, who has been thinking about death, and he has been asking me all sorts of practical questions.

"How do people get to Heaven, do they walk?"

He tossed out this particular query from the back seat of our rented Pontiac Firebird while we were driving to the Cape Breton Regional Hospital to visit his granny, who had told him two days previous—tremulous, clutching a rosary—that she expected to be in Heaven soon with her husband, Stan. This is not the sort of thing that I would generally encourage grandparents to say to five-year-olds, particularly when their mother has not yet prepared them for the concept of finite existence. But Lester took from it what he could, which is to say nothing, beyond the idea of Heaven itself as a new destination. Now Earth consists of four places: our summer cottage, Toronto, Cape Breton and Heaven.

The North Atlantic wind was buffeting the car, so cold that my earlobes were still throbbing in spite of the car's heater and I could barely keep my shivering hands still on the wheel.

"No, I don't think they walk to Heaven," I replied.

In truth, I haven't got the faintest idea how people get to Heaven. I have never read the Bible. Nor the Talmud, the Koran or the *Tibetan Book of the Dead*. If any of them have specified the transit route to the afterlife, I am simply unaware. So.

"They float," I told Lester, experimentally.

"They float?" He sounded awed. We passed Dana, my mother-in-law's cousin, who was shuffling along the icy sidewalk, head to the wind, with a bag of Kentucky Fried Chicken in the crook of her arm. I slowed down to wave. She pointed emphatically to the bag, and then uphill toward the hospital, indicating that she was on her way to deliver the contents to Bernice.

"Great," I mouthed to her, nodding.

"Do they float in the lake?" Lester asked.

"I beg your pardon?"

"When people go to Heaven, do they have to wear a life jacket?"

"No, they—I don't think they float on water, Lester, they float in the air. They don't float like fish, they float like leaves. Except up."

"Where, up?"

It's the follow-up questions that nail you. You can get away with fairly preposterous theories when you're talking to a five-year-old, but you have to have thought them through. Santa Claus, the Easter Bunny, the Tooth Fairy, the probable existence of elves: these are lines of inquiry that I've rehearsed. "Ah, the Tooth Fairy. Yes, she's very special, Lester," I was able to explain recently, when his friend Clarence turned up at the Tweedle Dee Daycare with a gap in his front teeth. "She wears a cloak of maple leaves and builds little castles made of teeth—deep in the forest. She'll leave coins under your pillow if you place your tooth there."

Ever since, Lester has been planning what to do with his windfall, and I have been silently adjusting the figure for tooth-fairy leavings depending upon what he envisions. Fifty cents doesn't buy much any more, but $4.99 is enough to snag a two-inch plastic hadrosaur at the Museum of Nature.

God is a different proposition entirely.

"I don't know where, exactly, they float," I conceded to my son. "Nobody knows, honey. The stairway to Heaven is a secret passage that only the dead can find."

For a moment I marveled at this impromptu theology until it hit me that I'd copped it from Led Zeppelin.

Lester was stuffing his nose into his ski mitt.

"Are we there yet?" he asked.

What saves you in the end is the fact that five-year-olds have no attention span.

"Don't worry, little goose," I said, because this one I knew: "We'll be there soon."

We were there, in fact, a minute later, for New Waterford is a teensy town on an enormous island in the North Atlantic, connected to mainland Nova Scotia by a single causeway. When I first came here with my boyfriend Calvin, more or less direct from New York City, I was amazed at the remoteness of the place, and further awed by the presence of malls. I could barely comprehend how piles of Mexican bananas and John Grisham novels could wend their way so far into the wilderness. Geography ought to have cast the island culturally adrift. Perhaps in some ways it had. Certainly nowhere else in North America had I seen fire hydrants painted as Smurfs.

The town Calvin comes from is inhabited by unemployed miners and their wives, all of whom work at the Cape Breton Regional Hospital serving tomato soup to the eldest of the unemployed miners, or next door at the Maple Hill Manor, serving soup to the eldest of the miners' wives. New Waterford was once a thriving community made prosperous by the Dominion Coal Company, which hired strapping young Acadians and Gaelic-speaking Scots to exhaust the motherlode while they sang. In the evening, they joined together to play their fiddles and accordions. At some point, as the mines closed and the miners began to pay for their careers with their lives, the business of the community shifted. Now, if you want to work here, your best bet is to learn how to give sponge baths.

As we got out of the car, I saw Dana's sister Janey trot through the squat brick hospital entrance and dart across the parking lot. I waved. She didn't see me, but waving is very important in New Waterford. I learned this on my maiden visit, when Calvin brought me to meet the unexpected grandparents of our unplanned child. I discovered that waving was far more essential than knowing who anyone was. Not waving signaled that you—the stranger, the New Yorker, in my case, for that was where I was living when I got pregnant—think you're too good for them. That you're stuck-up. A snob.

In fact, I feel quite the opposite here. I worry that Calvin's relations and all of their friends secretly think I'm inferior. Inept at baking, lousy at bingo, ill informed on the subjects that matter—like God, good coffee and how to craft doilies. Luckily, New Waterford folk are very kind, provided that you wave, and they have been a wonder in their care for my ailing eighty-year-old mother-in-law.

Bernice's condition has proved vexing to diagnose. It was clear when I arrived on Sunday night that she could neither walk nor breathe, which to me suggested something along the lines of dying. But I had no experience with serious illness—hats off to the hardy genes of Highland Scots, from whom I descend. "I got asthma and it's swellin' up my legs," Bernice explained, when she called Calvin a couple of weeks ago at our rented Toronto duplex. "Love a God, Calvin, this hospital is gonna be the death of me, they're makin' me eat fried baloney for lunch! Those nurses, they don't know what they're doing, they're just stuffin' me full a pills and needles. They don't know *what* they're doing."

"Well, what does Dr. Richardson say?" Calvin asked, hunched over on one of our mismatched kitchen chairs with his right hand covering his eyes.

"He's no use, the old goat," Bernice grumbled. "He don't even come in here, he's playing golf."

"It's December, Mum, he can't be playing golf."

"Darts, then. He don't come around, he's no use a'tall. My feet are all blown up. Can't fit my slippers."

Calvin sank lower in his chair and sighed. He refused to speculate with Bernice about what ailed her. He had an unwritten rule. Never speak of death to the possibly dying. Certainly not when the possibly dying refuse to acknowledge that they really are quite possibly dying, but keep insisting instead that they are back in hospital for the tenth time in two years with "a breathing spell," which, in itself, makes them constantly tearful. The merest hint in your voice suggesting a graver predicament prods them to half-shout, half-sob: "You think I'm done for, don't you!"

It's very tricky with Bernice.

Easier talking to her doctors, surely. I assumed that, when I got here, it would be a straightforward matter of saying, "So, what's going on?" Whereupon somebody in the medical profession would say, "Well, we have conducted 106 tests and the results tell us conclusively that Bernice has asthma and it's swelling up her legs."

But it turns out that if the patient herself cannot tell you what's going on, it is remarkably difficult to find out from doctors, who flee down the corridor like startled deer whenever someone they don't recognize approaches. And, without the nod from Dr. Richardson, the nurses were only prepared to divulge Bernice's moods, which ranged from "pretty good" on Monday, to "not so good" on Tuesday, with Wednesday as yet unknown.

Lester and I stamped into the pale-blue lobby, bringing the wind with us through the revolving door so that it ruffled the pages of Sue's magazine on the reception desk and prompted her to sit up straight and rub her arms.

"'Brrrr. How ya doin'?" she called, tamping down the magazine. "Dana was just in, hon."

Sue rarely needed to say, "May I help you?" as if she didn't know who she was addressing, which was a very sweet part of this deal. The New Waterford hospital was more like a club for hypochondriacs and dying people than a formal medical institution. The whole town was like a communal living room—the KFC, the drugstore, the Tim Hortons. By contrast, Torontonians had a tendency to pretend that they had never seen each other in their entire lives, even if they ran into one another daily. It had been puzzling me lately, for instance, that the guy at my local Starbucks persisted in acting as if he had no idea who I was, and could not anticipate that I would order my entirely predictable vanilla latte. I had started wondering if I should walk in one day with my hair shampooed into a stiffly lathered rhino horn, just to see if he said, "Oh, you've changed your look."

BELIEVE ME

The hospital lobby was quiet today, and you could tell Sue was up for a chat, but Lester had already said "Abracadabra," and reached up to push the elevator button. When the steel door creaked open, he darted in and whirled around, ready to say abracadabra again as we exited, obliging me to chase after him. The elevator lurched. I looked at the same Bingo for Breast Cancer fundraising notice that I'd been reading all week—the way at Bernice's house I kept absently perusing a framed needlepoint picture of a chubby kitten saying "Jesus is Purr-fect."

"Hi, handsome," said Barbara when we walked out onto the second floor. She bent down to squeeze Lester's nose. He covered it with his mitts and peered at her guardedly. Barbara straightened up, smiled indulgently, and smoothed her white nurse's tunic.

"Bernice is pretty good today, hon, " she told me, resolving the mystery of Wednesday. "Ate up all her breakfast this mornin'."

We walked into Room 12, and found Bernice in her bed, picking at a KFC drumstick and gingerly slurping Ensure. Lester pulled off his hat and flung it carelessly to the floor. Then he jutted out his arms scarecrow-style so that I could yank off his jacket. He studied his granny in her bed for a beat, and then asked her when she was going to die.

"In fifteen minutes?"

I prepared to drop to my knees and crawl out of the room unnoticed, but Lester was gazing at Bernice with such marvelous solemnity that it made her laugh, which plunged her into a coughing fit. She held her plump fist to her mouth and heaved herself onto her side, the pale-green sheet sliding off her hump of a back until her rayon nightie—lavender, extra large—was visible down to the hip. After clearing her throat a few times to be sure, she regained her composure and replied hoarsely, "No, God love us, dear. Not in fifteen minutes, I still haven't had my dessert."

She gave her silver rosary a perfunctory rub, and then reached over to the metal bedside table to grasp at a bag of gumdrops. Bernice and Lester have a very similar diet, I'd come to notice, except that one of them opts for savory junk, and the other for sweet. I suppose Bernice had been obliged by the sheer dreadfulness of hospital food to confine herself mostly to candy. It is one of life's enduring mysteries that the medical establishment can be so pompous about obesity and cancer and heart disease and their relation to diet, and then feed hospital patients meals with the nutritional value of J-Cloths.

On Monday morning, Bernice had lifted the plastic lid that covers plates on hospital trays—providing a little frisson of intrigue in the boring days of the chronically ill—and discovered a single slice of fried Spam. Inexplicably, this curled strip of lunch meat came accompanied by a tiny paper cup filled with brown sugar. To wash it all down she had received some tepid tap water in a cup, and a sad little tea bag.

We stared at this breakfast for a very long time, trying to determine its meaning. Had the hospital cooks given up serving toast, on account of the fact that steam-damp triangles of thin white bread invariably got boomeranged back to them from all corners of the Regional, so that the entire exercise of toasting, triangulating and serving the bread was deemed futile? Was the brown sugar supposed to be mixed into a forgotten bowl of oatmeal, or did the cooks rightly assume that Bernice wouldn't be able to digest a mush with the texture of wood pulp, so they skipped the oatmeal, yet provided the brown sugar as a sort of code, a clue to its absence? Was it a cry for help?

"Nine-one-one, how may I direct your call?"

"We are the cooks in the basement at the Cape Breton Regional Hospital, and management is forcing us to serve our patients hay."

You will be shocked to learn, as I was, that most hospitals employ a full-time dietician. Isn't that strange? Hospitals could hire a twelve-year-old boy to organize their menus during a commercial break from *Fear Factor* for a fraction of the cost of dieticians, and I feel fairly certain that he would come up with the same buttered Wonder Bread sandwich for lunch.

In any event, we waited for the food to go away, as was our custom, and then Lester and I meandered down to the kiosk in the lobby to buy the verboten fresh fruit and muffins that had yet to make an unsolicited appearance on a hospital breakfast tray.

In the meantime, Bernice ate sweets; in addition to the gumdrops, she had caramels, jujubes, Oreo cookies and Oh Henry! bars in her drawer, among which she had strewn blood-pressure tablets and hefty red capsules meant to soothe indigestion. These, the nurses gave her every morning, and these, every morning, she hid away. Yesterday, I discovered several in her running shoes under the bed.

"Why don't you tell them you don't have indigestion?" I asked, holding up a pill. She warded me off by shaking her head vigorously and scrunching her eyes shut, but I persisted. "And if you can't swallow the blood-pressure pill, you can take a liquid form—that's what they've been giving Julia."

Julia lay one bed over from Bernice on a custom-built air mattress that inflated or deflated depending upon how sore her back was. She was ninety-three, parked at the Regional with arthritis and a broken hip, and most of the time, she reclined in eerie stillness, at least a foot higher than anyone else in the room, as if arranged atop her own sarcophagus. She was dark and hirsute and hook-nosed— and when she laughed, it was soundless, her dried-up mouth stretching at the corners as her brittle body shook.

"Go on, Bernice," she'd said yesterday, her voice a croaked whisper. "You stuff yourself so much you could eat the lamb of God, so what's wrong with a cup of Gaviscon?"

My impulse was to nod in agreement: *exactly*, but then I paused midway through wagging my chin. Better to stay clear of that remark? "I'll check with Barbara," I said, looking futilely around before restoring Bernice's pill to her shoe.

"Momma," asked Lester, "is the granny in that bed going to die too?"

"Jeez Louise, Les, will you stop being so morbid?" I hissed.

But Julia, sharp-eared, gave that soundless laugh of hers. I suppose it's not so frightening to be quizzed about death by a child. Not when you're Julia's age. We thirty- and forty-somethings are the haunted ones, between the very young and the very old, who would rather die than talk about it.

Here are some of the discussions I have had with my son about death:

Squashed squirrel in throes of rigor mortis appears on sidewalk, looking different, somehow, than other squirrels. "Why, Momma?"
Sleeping.

Lion chews off antelope's head on Discovery Channel nature show.
Just playing.

Bambi. Mother shot. Mother absent. OH NOOOOO!
Bad men attacked mother with guns, made her . . . sick. Went to deer hospital.

Grandfather Stan dies of heart attack. Might be definitive moment to explain death to child, but Momma and Daddy postpone mentioning that it happened.
Never mind.

*   *   *

Indeed, Momma and Daddy noticed that their friends and aquaintances had a hard time talking about the death of Calvin's father, too. Not that it was emotionally difficult for them of course, but they didn't seem to be comfortable with the vocabulary of grief. What does one say, after all, when the reassuring remark of earlier decades—"He's with God now"—can no longer be universally accepted or assumed?

"Sorry to hear about your dad, man," muttered various musicians. My mother added, ever practical: "It's important to let the sadness wash through you, Calvin, don't bottle it up." Like this was all about him, or them. There were no longer the words to suggest that it had been about Stan.

2

"I'd better come out there, Mum," Calvin had offered two weeks ago, after Dana phoned to reinforce the message that Bernice was, indeed, hospitalized with swollen legs and who knew what else, moose pox maybe.

"Oh no, dear," Bernice had wanly protested. "No, no, no. You can't afford the air fare. Better to wait until I'm home and can make you a proper supper."

Lately, Bernice had been more adamant than ever that she wasn't too good, but that we could not, under any circumstances, come to see her. She didn't want us to witness her all swollen up and wheezing, with her white hair tufted and askew. She knew we would let her carry on this way indefinitely, shooing us off with remarks about airfare, hell-bent on recovering her health and dignity and returning home to make meat pies. But Dana's phone call was unprecedented—who knows how she even got our number? After hanging up, Calvin and I sat at our kitchen table, he with a can of Double Diamond and me with some merlot in a juice glass. We eyed each other and allowed: here's the shit, and here's the fan.

A prolonged silence followed. Easily five minutes. I listened to our neighbor's Great Dane barking. The couple next door began shouting, which came through the wall in muffled sing-song tones. They're a pair of Italians who argue easily and almost impersonally, whereas Calvin and I, being equal parts repressed Catholic and reticent WASP, do not clash with angry voices. Instead, we ineffectually stab at one other with pointed looks. An escalation in conflict between us entails moving from sighs and dueling eyes to unheralded refusals to do things around the house, like washing the dishes or serving a more appetizing meal than Tuna Helper.

I wouldn't recommend this to other couples as a strategy for marital combat, if only because it depends upon the other person actually noticing. Once, when Calvin was mad at me for staying out until dawn with some friends, an entire fortnight went by before I realized that he had ever been mad at me, and this *anger* was the reason he no longer took out the garbage.

On the subject of his ailing mother, we engaged in a knock-down, drag-out exchange of looks rendered absolutely electric by our shared guilt.

"You, you, you," I jabbed at him with piercing eyes. "It's *your* mother. If my parents were sick, I would be with them in a flash." Of course, that was easy to say since they lived about ten blocks away in robust health.

"No, you," he retorted by way of a glare.

"Why me?" My eyes flashed. The new mommy had been elected to care for the old one? Is that what he was saying? The dog carried on outside, barking pompously at nothing. I poured another cup of wine. Glanced at my watch. Sighed loudly, and finally broke the silence: "Come on, Calvin, there is no one else to see her through this, and it's almost Christmas."

Bernice's sister Shirley had gone down to Florida for the winter, where she was deeply involved in the Jacksonville Golden Years Bingo tournament. President of the organizing committee. A sudden revelation of purpose, after life-long drift. As much as she loved her sister, she knew Bernice's history of hypochondria and would need to see a death certificate before she'd abandon the action.

"Don't you think your mother needs family?" I asked. "If not hanging around keeping her company, then at least to find out what's actually wrong with her?"

Calvin laid his head down flat on the table, so that the cowlick in his nut-brown hair popped up and danced to and fro. When he gazed up at me again, his eyes were misted over, the closest he'd ever come to tears. "I can't deal with my mother," he muttered, "not this soon after Dad." Stan died—boom—from a heart attack right in the middle of the Stanley Cup playoffs just this past May. Still spry and self-sufficient up to that point, and then off he went, without preamble. Living, reachable by phone, chuckling at Bernice, and then gone. Calvin had to organize the funeral, which Bernice refused to attend, bawling

17

that she couldn't bear it. Calvin never talks about it now, although at the time, he told me how strange it was, to walk home from the hospital with his dad's spectacles in his pocket, thinking, what should he do with them, should he donate them, and then realizing, stopped rigid on King Street, that they were now the most useless things in the world.

The way I have come to understand these things, a scant five years into my relationship with Calvin, is that lovers take turns getting haunted and freaked out by the challenges that life scares up. It's only fair.

The following morning, I booked Lester and me a flight.

3

I have only ever been in hospital twice. Once, to come into the world all soggy and squalling, and the next time to usher in my son. In neither case was my stay long, so I was intrigued by the idea of Bernice sharing a room with several incapacitated roommates, all of whom took great interest in one another, as if they were girls at boarding school.

Life in Room 12 was a multi-generational affair. In addition to Julia and Bernice, there was jolly Aileen—who went on a package tour to the Yucatán and managed to fall off a Mayan pyramid, which apparently happens to several tourists each year. She had smashed her knee in her tumble down the side of the ruin, and after immediate care by Mexican doctors, wound up here to recuperate.

Aileen was sixty or so, and shared her side of the room with Celia, who was only twenty-five. Celia had gotten married the previous summer, and her young husband, Joe, came to see her twice a day, bringing Chinese food and DoodleArt posters, with a fresh box of markers each weekend. She always looked up at him and smiled with grateful love, as if she could not believe that a man would take such a leap of faith as to entwine himself with an invalid. Celia was in chronic pain from an unsuccessful scoliosis operation, a procedure she was preparing, once again, to endure.

Lester had taken to sitting cross-legged on her bed, coloring his socks with her markers. I sat on a little fold-out chair beside Bernice, who alternately dozed, stared about dully, wept, and gossiped about everybody else in the room. When a nurse wheeled Julia outside and downstairs for a smoke, Bernice whispered to me loudly that Julia was the richest pensioner on Cape Breton Island.

"That bed cost her twenty-five thousand dollars!" she exclaimed, hauling herself up to a sitting position with the zest of her conviction.

I wondered whether to point out that the richest pensioner on Cape Breton Island could probably buy themselves a private hospital room. But I was just there to listen, I felt. Being a coal miner's widow, Bernice was not familiar with what wealth could afford, and drew her own conclusions. The yardstick she tended to use was the purchase of appliances. If you had a pressure cooker, but you also bought a microwave oven on sale at the Mayflower Mall, then you could walk with your head held high. Dana had just acquired a deep-fryer, which raised her considerably in Bernice's estimation. Carol, her next-door neighbor, had a portable paper shredder, which put her on a par with the queen of England.

"Does she have a lot of papers to shred, do you find?" I asked in puzzlement.

"It's all them forms from the *government*," Bernice explained.

I nodded. Julia with her inflatable hospital bed was the *ne plus ultra*.

In a way, this subject of appliances was a difficult one for me and Bernice, because I didn't have any. Calvin and I were paupers, without a waffle-maker to show for our strivings, and she knew that. So she stepped lightly around the subject, trying her best not to upset me by prying. Since she couldn't think of what else to ask me, there tended to be gaps in her sense of who I was. She still called me Nancy, for instance, which isn't my name.

"It's Frannie, Mum," Calvin had told her repeatedly. "Nancy's your cousin in Montreal."

"Oh, Lord in Heaven, I'm sorry," Bernice would say. And then do it again the very next time we talked.

Celia had produced some cerise nail polish, and was carefully painting her nails. She had agreeably dabbed bite wounds on the ribs of Lester's plastic triceratops first, and he was playing with it now, plunging it into death throes in the tangle of her sheet.

"You got a date today, hon?" asked Aileen, gazing up from her paperback novel.

"Joe's pickin' me up in an hour. He's takin' me to the Cranberry Nook for lunch." Celia looked pleased, but she had deep shadows under her eyes, and a sheen of perspiration on her forehead.

"You need any help?" I asked.

"Naw, I'm okay," she demurred. Then she thought about it, waving her nails dry. "Actually, maybe you could help wheel me to the bathroom to do up my hair?"

The harsh bathroom light was unflattering to both of us. Celia looked twice as ill, and I looked fat. The smell of disinfectant was nauseating. I ran a brush carefully through her lank brown hair.

"You know," she said, somewhat tentatively, "I had asthma real bad as a kid, and it never swelled up my legs."

I nodded. Bernice's explanation for being in hospital was somewhat akin to my claiming that the reason I had put on weight was because I had rickets.

Celia peered up at me in the toothpaste-spattered mirror, her head gently bobbing backwards as I brushed. "What does Dr. Richardson say about her taking sick like that, with asthma?"

"I still haven't seen him," I said, smiling, and Celia rolled her eyes and murmured, "My God, that man should not earn a paycheck."

"I probably shouldn't be telling you this," she added, "but Barbara told me that Bernice had arm cancer."

"Oh," I said.

Actually, for years, Bernice had told everybody she had arm cancer, which—I explained to Celia—doesn't exist, technically, as a medical condition. She had struggled with breast cancer about a decade ago, and had had a radical mastectomy to wrench herself free of the disease. Ever since, she had chosen to interpret everything from stomach acid to the knotty cysts of old age as cancer's return. This had made chatting with her by telephone every Sunday from Toronto a somewhat surreal experience. In most families, I am assuming, news of terminal cancer gets broken only once.

The time she reported an inoperable liver tumor we canceled our plans to attend a friend's wedding in New York in order to go out to see her. The liver cancer, however, either never progressed or was entirely invented, for it ebbed out of her monologues some months later, supplanted by the announcement that she had cancer in her neck.

I got so used to Bernice's baffling declarations, interspersed as they were with increasingly wild suspicions about Dana thieving her lawn ornaments and Archie the yard man conspiring to steal her new Garden Weasel, that it all became a blur. It was impossible to suss her out. After Stan died, Bernice rarely left her house, only venturing into Sydney to shop at sales, as enervated yet compelled as a starving hunter heading into the jungle. She blamed her inertia on coughs and colds and headaches and dizzy spells. In the grip of her aging and her fear, she could not be persuaded to come to see us in Toronto.

"Oh no, dear," she said to Calvin, turning his invitation down once again this summer. "The only places I'm headed now are Mayflower Mall and the grave."

Calvin and I are not take-charge people. We tend to be more the run-away-in-bewilderment type. It's nice to share traits with your life partner, but in this case something more complementary probably would have come in handy. Calvin's disinclination to deal with his mother had to do with having grown up with her. But I rode with it—*"What?* You aren't going to insist that we spend the holidays in New Waterford with your mother talking about arm cancer?"—and I never pushed Calvin to go.

I couldn't explain all of this to Celia. It was my own problem, I figured, the bad-daughter-in-law guilt I was feeling now like a whup upside the head.

"You look pretty as a June rose today, hon," Aileen exclaimed when I wheeled Celia back out of the bathroom sporting a lopsided french twist. She lit up and said: "Oh go on, I'm young, that's all you're jealous of."

"You got a be-oootiful bun," Bernice piped in.

"Don't know what good it'll do me," Celia complained, "with this pain I'm feelin.'"

"Least you had a honeymoon before you come in here," Julia muttered. "Charlie was the first Cape Breton Highlander to go over to It'ly and the first to come back in a chair. I never got to have the you-know-what, not all my life, I never had a spasm."

There was a moment of shocked silence in the room, then Celia and I brayed with laughter. When you're ninety-three, what the hell do you care? Is that not so? Maybe you're thinking that you've been good all your life, and you've gained entry to the Kingdom of Heaven. Now you can safely rue what you've missed.

4

On Wednesday afternoon I spotted Bernice's doctor leaning against the counter of the nurses' station, not thirty feet away. "Oh! Dr. Richardson!" I shouted, like a winning contestant on *The Price Is Right*. He didn't hear me. I began to trot forward. Richardson was eighty-four years old, and he creaked about in buffed black shoes, stoop-shouldered and shaky. He had a hearing aid, which drove Bernice up the wall because, in her view, it lent him a false sense of confidence. She couldn't project her voice any more, and between her ailment and his deafness, they tended to have exceedingly peculiar conversations. The last time I was out here visiting, I observed an exchange between them that went something like this:

"My arm cancer's spread, hasn't it?"

"Alarm? No, no, no need for alarm, Bernice."

"Am I done for then, or not?"

"Oh no, oh no, I haven't used camphor as a medicine in years. We'll give you something much more up to date, Bernice, don't you worry a'tall."

Dr. Richardson would go down with the Regional, that was the consensus. No use hiring someone new when the place had been slated for closure by the provincial government. He had acted as New Waterford's GP for sixty years, and now presided over the emergency room, which would be highly alarming in Chicago or Toronto, but less so here, since everyone *knew* that Dr. Richardson presided over the ER, and paramedics took real emergencies to the hospital in nearby Sydney.

I tapped him on his bony shoulder, so that he turned away from Barbara and regarded me uncertainly through his glasses.

"Dr. Richardson, I'm Frannie Mackenzie, Bernice Puddie's daughter-in-law?"

"Ah yes, ah yes, nice to meet you." He replaced his pen in the pocket of his white coat and offered me his trembling hand.

"I've come out to see her from Toronto and . . . but I'm not actually sure what her diagnosis is. So—" I smiled apologetically.

He interlocked his fingers and held them at chest level.

"I beg your pardon, dear?"

We were two doors down from Bernice's room. I was extremely disinclined to speak up.

"What is wrong with my mother-in-law?" I asked, raising my voice one tense notch.

He smiled vaguely, and I wasn't sure whether he had heard me, but then he opined: "She's not too good. Not too good. I'm afraid the chickens are coming home to roost."

"Are you saying that her cancer has spread?"

"I'm sorry?"

I shut my eyes, crossed my fingers, and achieved something slightly less conspicuous than a bellow: "Has her cancer spread?"

Celia reappeared from the patient snack room with Lester, who was sipping from a cup of Coke the size of his head. They started toward us.

"Bernice's best days are behind her. It's safe to say that the crows are gathering on the wire, it is certainly safe to say that."

"Mommy, there's a *bee* in the snack room, I saw it!" Lester bolted toward me and, in his excitement, slipped and did a face-plant, spilling his Coke, which spread out in yard-long rivulets. By the time I had rescued him, toweled off his pants, dried his tears and replaced his drink, it was safe to say that Richardson had flown the coop.

5

"Can we have Kentucky chicken?" Lester asked as we passed by the franchise on the way home from the Regional.

"You know what? You've had that for the last two nights. What you have to do, small boy, is vary your diet. If you don't eat fruit or vegetables you won't grow."

"Why?" He kicked the back of my seat with his Blue's Clues boots, fidgety.

"Because you can't grow tall and strong on french fries. You need other things too. "

"Like pie?"

I pulled the car into Bernice's driveway and turned off the ignition. I didn't want to go into the little aluminum-sided house, empty as a motel suite. "I'll take you out for supper, but we're not going to Kentucky Fried Chicken. We'll go to the tavern part of Room with a Cue."

In the cavernous, half-filled pool hall, Lester ate a grilled cheese sandwich and finger-painted with his ketchup, while I drank beer and gnawed on my predicament. The unexpected confusion was making me tense. What was I bracing Lester for? What was I going to tell Calvin, who was recording an album at the CBC studios in Toronto with his new jazz trio consisting of marimba, violin and kazoo? What if I had to stay here indefinitely? How could I deal with all the contingencies with no real information? I was very close to blurting out to Bernice, "So, are you dying, or what?" Which would have obliged me to flee New Waterford at once.

Could we airlift her to Toronto like sedated livestock on a sling? That seemed shockingly cruel—import her to a more convenient milieu, and set up a death watch for her on the futon. But the alternative was to move here. To pull up Lester's tender roots and mine, quit my job and hunker down against a cold Atlantic wind that reeked of coal. There are things you can do for the people you love that are harder to contemplate for people who call you Nancy.

I signaled the waitress for another Moosehead lager. Of course, I could pull it off if I had to. Motherhood had taught me nothing less. I could have my work sent to me, and edit at Bernice's kitchen table. The question of home-editing the *Dandelion Review*—Canada's only book-review monthly—from out here was only an issue when it came to thinking about what to do with my son.

I had tried working at home when Lester was smaller, and really, I did not understand the meaning of the word "hampered" until I began taking business calls with a fifteen-month-old underfoot.

"Hello?"

"Hello, Ms. Mackenzie, this is—"

"Will you excuse me for a moment? Lester! Take that out of your mouth right now. Spit it out."

"Ms. Mackenzie, I'm just returning your—"

"I'm sorry, can you hang on? I *will* get you a Fruit Roll-Up in a *minute!*"

"Anyway, I thought—"

"Lester, don't press that button, you'll hang up the—"

BEEEEEEP—BEEP-BEEP-BEEP—

This is the meaning of the word "hampered."

Far braver and stronger women than I am are actually being work-at-home moms voluntarily all over North America, to the point where it's become a sort of movement—with chat groups and conventions and newsletters. How viable is that? Are there sins of omission being committed in the stories of triumph, wherein Judy So-and-So of Louisville claims to pull off a six-figure salary as a wool-diaper-cover designer with three kids in the house? I wonder, because when you phone someone at work, and their assistant says they're "in a meeting," what they would have meant in my case was that I was trapped in the bathroom, where I couldn't get up from the toilet because Lester wouldn't let go of my leg. If I stood up to pry him loose, he would immediately plunge his hand into the toilet, so that I wouldn't be able to fling my arm back fast enough to flush, and there we would be for hours, practically, involved in an absurd Mexican stand-off.

31

"I'm sorry," my receptionist would have had to say, "Ms. Mackenzie is unable to wipe her own ass at the moment, may I take a message?"

The work-at-home-mom thing lasted for ten stunningly unproductive months, after which I banished Lester to Tweedle Dee Daycare. A few months ago, Calvin got a taste of what I'd been complaining about when he agreed to be interviewed by BBC Radio in London while Lester was at home with a case of lice. Calvin was in the kitchen, discoursing expertly on the illustrious career of Gim Knutson, just deceased, an experimental jazz musician who had pioneered the use of electrified windshield wipers in improvisational quartets, when Lester picked up the phone in our bedroom.

"Who are you talking to, Daddy?" he inquired, live on air.

"Lester, hang up please, sweetie, I'll be done in a minute."

"Hi, Granddaddy."

"Lester, it isn't Granddaddy, please get off the phone."

"Can I have a cow piñata?"

"Yes, you can have a piñata, but only if you get off the phone."

"Okay."

"Lester?"

"Hi, Daddy."

Children hamper professional life, it seems to me, because they remind you how much you're pretending.

"Can I have another Coke?" Lester asked me now, as if I hadn't sailed off in my head to the land where the wild things are, and had been sitting there this whole time, alertly watching him achieve a work of genius with a condiment.

"No."

"Pleeeeease? Can I have a Sprite then?"

I cupped my chin in one hand and smiled. Lester's face is long and narrow, unusually so for a small child. It must have something to do with his diet of carbohydrates and air. With his flat bangs and collar-length chestnut hair, I often think that he resembles the actor Christopher Guest, playing that earnest heavy-metal guitarist in *This Is Spinal Tap*. Nigel Tufnel. "It goes to eleven." There is something in Lester's look—a combination of innocence, gravitas and helmet hair—that makes me laugh.

"What about ice cream instead?" I asked.

"Yesss! Okay! Yesss!" Like he'd won the lottery.

Not that he'd eat it.

I waved over the waitress, and when she delivered two scoops of strawberry in an odd metal dish, Lester grew quickly absorbed in the task of ice-cream–sculpting with a straw and a butter knife. At some point, I had discovered that children approach eating as an arts-and-crafts activity. What do you want to do today, Lester? Go to the museum, or suck icing through a straw?

The revelation was extremely liberating, in that it often freed me to muse or make phone calls. Or fret. I had a great deal of fretting to catch up on, it seemed to me, and most of it sprang from the task on the table just now.

6

"So, how is she?" Calvin shouted into a pay phone later that night. He was at the Horseshoe Tavern in Toronto, watching a show. I could barely hear him over the hubbub. It made me feel lonely. I was sitting at Bernice's plastic-covered dining room table in a silence so complete that it seemed to hum, staring at a jar of twinkly-wrapped toffees and a vase full of plastic roses.

"Well," I began—how to explain?—"the chickens have come home to roost and the cows are in the barn."

"What are you talking about?"

"I have no idea! I finally ran into Dr. Richardson, and that is what he told me. I was going to ask him if he could be a little more specific but Lester distracted me."

On the other end of the phone, a French horn wailed and someone demanded a Pilsner.

"If it's any help," I added, "the nurse says she's

doin' pretty good, and she ate all her lunch today."

"Jesus," said Calvin, "that's nothing new. My mother could be thrown from an airplane and still eat all her lunch. What about Dr. Pereira? Didn't he run some tests at that oncology clinic in Sydney?"

Dr. Pereira was a refreshingly straightforward guy, one of two cancer specialists in Cape Breton. It was odd that there were only two, given how many people on the island had cancer, either from the environmental disaster out at the Sydney Tar Ponds, or from coal-mining or smoking. In any event, Pereira was an immigrant from Sri Lanka who evidently preferred being called "the Paki" by Bernice and her elderly ilk to being blown up by Tamil Tigers in Columbo.

"I'm waiting to hear from him," I told Calvin. I carried the portable phone into the kitchen, opening and closing drawers in search of a corkscrew. "Apparently they lost the test results in Sydney and he still has to review them, assuming that they find them, before he talks to me. Where does your mother keep her corkscrew?"

"She doesn't have one. They didn't drink."

Oh, bleh.

"So what do you want me to do?" I asked.

"Can you just stay there for a bit longer? Bill had to reschedule the recording session next week. Rick Mercer's in the studio doing some sort of Christmas special. Just hang out with her until we get the results, at least?"

"What about Christmas?"

"We'll figure it out. I'll come out there, or you guys can come back here, or . . . oh, I don't know. Fuck."

That night, I dreamt my father told me that I got a new editing job, a fantastic one at a famous magazine, but he couldn't remember which one, which magazine had called and left the message. All he knew was that I had to audition. I was to arrive costumed in a bell-shaped coat made of cast iron, and wear a chef's hat.

"But why?"

"Otherwise, they're giving the job to Calvin," my father said. "That's all I know."

It is disconcerting to sleep in the house of your in-laws when one has vanished entirely and the other might never return. There is a sense of haunting, and of trespass, like being in a theater after the play has ended but before the set has been struck. Everything in the little aluminum-sided dwelling on Plummer Avenue remained in place—two La-Z-Boy chairs covered in doilies, a list of important phone numbers taped to the living room wall, Stan's beloved wide-screen TV, his final *National Enquirer*, a bowl of wrinkled oranges, a radio tuned to some golden oldies station. But no one presiding. Only a lingering smell of sickness, the indefinable scent of someone old.

Lester's response to this curious sensation was to transform his grandparents' house into a diorama from the Cretaceous period. Within days of our arrival, a plastic lambeosaur had been seated in one La-Z-Boy and a plush maiasaur in the other. A small herd of brachiosaurs marched across the mantelpiece. Two velociraptors guarded the toaster in the kitchen, an allosaurus ascended the stairs in pursuit of a fallen-over goat, and a basilosaurus—famed reptilian predator of the prehistoric oceans—bobbed in the guestroom toilet.

I was a guilty co-conspirator in this transformation, if only because I kept putting Bernice's things away to fend off any accidents. When we walked in the first night, I found blood-pressure pills scattered about like the Reese's Pieces in *E.T.* and had to crouch and dart with a Dirt Devil, one step ahead of Lester, who yearned to follow the path of the candy-red pills and pop them in his mouth. Also hoovered up or swept to higher perches were bottles of tranquilizers, Imodium, tamoxifen, steroids, baggies of codeine.

And then, by increments, the gadgets and geegaws of the elderly: half-empty Depends boxes, an oxygen mask, bathrobes, cans of Ensure, a blood-pressure gauge. I feared that Lester would engage in ad hoc adaptations, just as Calvin once used Bernice's sanitary napkin as a hammock for his G.I. Joe. The potential for an absurd and embarrassing reassignment of function to every object in the house seemed almost limitless. So, over the course of days, the playthings of a five-year-old took over the space, while the accoutrements of the eighty-year-old disappeared. By the end of the week, I had even removed such benign knickknacks as a miniature toilet bowl down which one flushed pennies, and a covered chuck-wagon drawn by ceramic horses.

"Lester," I protested, when I rescued the chuckwagon, "stop playing with that. It isn't a toy."

He stared at me, uncomprehending.

"It's not for touching, it's for looking at."

"Why?"

"*Why?*" I ran my hands through my hair, trying to imagine the purpose of simply gazing at the thing as an object. I am not a collector. Not of that kind. I do collect quite a lot of clutter at home in Toronto, but that's because I'm afraid to throw things out. There's this small red domino, for instance, that's been sitting on the floor of my living room for a couple of months. I come across it every now and then and ponder what to do with it. I know it belongs to a set of dominoes that someone gave to Lester. I can't remember where the other dominoes are, and it's not like I have a drawer in my kitchen that I can label "One Lost Domino." There's no obvious place for it to reside that I can think of, other than the box that it came in, which I'm positive is around somewhere. I occasionally come home from Ikea with little storage containers in pastel colors, but they wind up containing one lost domino, a shoelace, some triple-A batteries, two takeout menus, a bicycle key and a flashlight, and to me that doesn't count as an improvement.

Thus, I had no explanation for my son about why he couldn't play with the chuckwagon, since I couldn't conceive of the purpose of deliberately collecting things. I merely declared, "Because it's not a toy, it's a thing. It's one of your grandmother's *things*."

Lester ducked his head. Was he getting in trouble?

"No, honey, it's not that, no."

"Maybe it's better that way," my friend Avery said when he called on Friday night. Lester was slurping turkey-rice soup at the kitchen table, and I was tugging at a bottle of wine with a weakly functioning corkscrew I'd picked up at the New Waterford Dollarama.

"What do you mean, better?" I asked.

"Well, consider that you have no history there. You can't attach any sentimental value to these objects, so the worst thing you feel is that you need to keep Lester from damaging them."

"That's actually not the worst thing I feel," I ventured, pouring the wine. "The worst thing I feel is that I'm sitting in the middle of an imminent garage sale."

I felt laden, indeed, with the knowledge that these things were about to be orphaned, if not by death then almost certainly by a move into the Maple Hill Manor nursing home. Stan was gone, Shirley was absent and Calvin was an only child. "These things are probably going to become *our* things, do you know what I mean? So every time I handle something that I realize I could use in Toronto, like this unopened box of kitchen knives I found in the cupboard, just *the fact* that I consider their future utility makes me feel like a vulture. It's horrible. It's like I've developed this little tic . . . like, this *greed* tic."

"A greed tic?" Avery sounded amused.

"Oh, whatever. You know what I mean."

"Well then, don't consider their future use."

"Thanks, Avery, that helps." I handed Lester a cupcake.

"But the opposite scenario is more traumatic, Frannie, which is the trouble most people have letting *go* of things. My uncle died over a year ago, and my cousins still haven't cleaned out his house, much less sold it. In fact, they've inadvertently rendered it spooky. There are cobwebs about, that sort of thing."

"Well, that's vivid. But it's also the point, Avery," I argued. "Most people feel an emotional connection, and I'm not talking about nostalgia, I'm talking about the world ending. That kind of emotional connection? And here I am, in this little house, and I don't feel *any*thing. No sentimental memory at all. Just this sudden stewardship of stuff. So, okay, it may *not* be worse than the other way around, but I'll stand by odd."

"Hmm," Avery mused. "Perhaps you would welcome a distraction, then. At least I hope so, because I need to send you a list of books to assign for review over Christmas."

Avery was my associate editor at the *Dandelion Review,* holding down our penniless tree-fort in Toronto. I owed him tons.

"Okay," I said, trying not to sigh audibly. "Like what?"

"Well, there's a coffee-table book coming out by a Quebec photographer, called *Cows of Vermont.*"

"You want us to review a collection of cow pictures?"

"Bear with me. I thought—if I could find a book to pair it with—it could make a nice essay on how colonialized we are in publishing, how we can't photograph *The Cows of the Eastern Townships* or *Cows of Quebec* without forfeiting an American contract. Has to be Vermont cows, that sort of thing."

"Oh, come on, Avery, are we that hard up for a good conversation?"

"Well, there's global warming."

"What else?"

"Okay. A new book coming out on what's called 'the science of irrationality.' How to profit from it, or something like that. And—just one second, let me see. Alright: two more biographies of Conrad Black, and another one on Earle Birney."

"Anything about Santa Claus and religion?"

"Uh . . . no."

I finished my wine, poured another glass. Gave Lester a cup of milk.

"Fine," I sighed. "Just send me the list."

Misery loves company, and so, it emerges, does Bernice's cousin Dana. She popped in on Saturday morning with a bagful of Tim Hortons coffee and two dozen sugar-glazed Timbits. Lester went off to watch PBS Kids in the living room with his hands full of Timbits while Dana and I settled ourselves at the table in Bernice's cheery little kitchen. I sipped my coffee and watched in silence while Dana's greedy eyes roamed unabashedly over the appliances.

"Don't mind if I smoke, do ya?" she asked. "God love Bernice, she gives me a right hard time about it. On account of her breathing." Dana pulled a packet of du Mauriers out of her parka and offered me one. I shook my head. She retrieved an ashtray from another pocket and placed it on the table before shrugging off her coat and running a hand through her short-cropped hair. "What do bin Laden and a pair a pantyhose have in common?" she asked.

"I beg your pardon?"

"*What* do bin Laden and pantyhose have in *common?*"

"Oh," I shrugged. "I don't know."

"They both agitate the Bush."

She delivered the punchline so wryly, as she lit her cigarette and exhaled between thin lips, studying me through hard gray eyes, that I wondered if the joke had something to do with being here together in Bernice Puddie's house. A grim inside joke that should cause us both to nod at one another with small, sad smiles. But . . . I waited, face frozen with my mouth half open, my bum tense . . . no?

"Oh, that's pretty good," I offered after a beat. "I can never remember jokes."

"So," Dana ventured, flicking ashes, "what did Richardson tell ya? I hear from Barbara that Bernice isn't doing too good, but I coulda told you that. She's been lyin in bed aa'll day for months. I come in here cleanin', make her soup, and she only gets up for that, then right back to bed. It's Stan what's done it to her. A broken heart, that's what brought back her arm cancer."

I considered this. "To tell you the truth, Richardson didn't give me a very clear picture, I don't actually— what makes you think her cancer is back?"

"Oh, I don't know that, hon," Dana genially conceded, sitting back and crossing her arms, "but just take one look at her, eh, blown up like that, so's her feet look like hockey mitts. If that's asthma, I'm Madonna."

"True," I agreed glumly, and sipped my coffee. From the living room, I could hear the intro song for *Dragon*

Tales, a breezy pair of female voices singing in harmony: "Come on now, take my hand, it's time to go to Dragonland." Now I was going to have that stuck in my head for the rest of the day. They work in rotation, these children's songs that stick in my head. Yesterday, for instance, it was the theme song from *Elliot Moose*. Even as I was combing Celia's hair and pondering her pallor, the pain she had to live with, the fate of my mother-in-law, the soundtrack in my head was going: "Elliot Moose, de dum de dum, is on the loose . . ."

I tend to think that there must be millions of working men and women with this Problem That Has No Name, which is that they spend the majority of their professional hours secretly singing Disney songs to themselves, sitting at their desks, driving forklifts, riding elevators and entering boardrooms all over North America, silently humming "*Hi* diddle-dee-dee, an actor's life for me." Truly, I like to imagine that there's a sleek, six-foot man at a Madison Avenue ad agency who, even as I write, is waiting for a major client to come in for a pitch about how to promote tuna fish or something and he can't help it, he's singing to himself, "Ariel's coming, Ariel's COMING!" from *The Little Mermaid II*. Meanwhile, a steely stockbroker like Sigourney Weaver's character in *Working Girl* is conducting a major sell-off of bonds on Wall Street whilst humming the high-pitched, fake-Oriental instrumental theme song from *Sagwa, the Chinese Siamese Cat*: "Da da da, nanananana, da da DA da da daa daa daa . . ."

It can't just be me and Calvin who get these songs

stuck in our heads. Or maybe it is, and that's why we don't have jobs on Madison Avenue and Wall Street.

"So what do you think you'll do with Bernice and Stan's watercooler when Bernice passes?" asked Dana, firing up another cigarette.

"Her watercooler?" I echoed, perplexed.

"You haven't seen it, hon? It's right behind ya! I fixed it for her last summer, and she told me if she ever took sick for good, I could have it, because what good would a water-cooler be, fightin' cancer?"

"Well, that's a point," I offered, tentative, "but it's not really up to me, I don't think. Bernice will talk to Calvin, or Shirley, when . . . you know . . . when it gets to that stage."

Dana regarded me with something like mirth, and then snorted. "Bernice isn't gonna admit she's dyin,' Frannie, not even when you're ready to wheel her to the morgue. She's just gonna keep on complainin' and carryin' on about how sick she is until one day God agrees with her."

7

It turns out that there are a limited number of activities for small children in hospitals. Lester blew through his options in our first week. His to-do list looked something like this:

Examine Grandmother's oxygen mask, and experiment with it as a suitable helmet for Sir Ruff the Dinosaur Hunter, until Momma freaks out.

Visit vending-machine room repeatedly, investigating how much ice can be made to tumble into one's cup, and after that into one's toque, and after that onto the floor.

Plea for rides in wheelchairs. When no one is looking, attempt to push wheelchair down the corridor and crash into someone's IV pole.

BELIEVE ME

Wander into strangers' rooms and gawk like a junior Lookie Loo as patients are administered injections, CPR or a sponge bath.

Crawl under beds and pretend that you're a panther, waiting for a choice moment to attack the unsuspecting, crepe-soled feet of nurses.

Die of boredom, and beg Momma to take you home. "Please?"

Calvin agreed to come out for Christmas, and this, in turn, persuaded Bernice to spend the holiday in her own house. It was a good idea, although somewhat fraught. She was enormously terrified of being more than ten feet from a nurse, for one thing. While she claimed to despise being in the hospital, wouldn't take her pills, and kept minimizing her illness, she clearly felt safer there. With good reason. I had forgotten where I'd put her blood-pressure gauge, and had absolutely no idea where I'd stuffed the extra package of Depends. In any event, she had no intention of going anywhere until her son personally escorted her, and in the meantime I set about trying to decorate her house.

Bernice, I discovered, had roughly eleven hundred battery-operated holiday ornaments, which made it quite easy for me to proceed. I assigned a wreath to the door, a foot-high spinning angel that sang "Joy to the World" to the living room window, and for the TV, a Santa Claus that climbed up and down a chimney, up and down and up and down, like an inexplicably jolly

Sisyphus. I found them in her wide-open, dust-free basement, in seven boxes marked XMAS. All of the boxes were stacked neatly between two deep freezers packed with jars of homemade jam, cabbage rolls, pork pies, turkey-rice soup and spaghetti sauce. On the other side of the freezers was a cupboard containing, unexpectedly, a dark mink coat. I wondered if it would be fair to consider these things together as the sum of a life in objects. Singing elves, provisions to ward off starvation lest Cape Breton's cranberry bogs fail, and elegant apparel for a long-lost girl who wanted to look swell and maybe even did, once, before she abandoned fashion for the vanities of illness.

I was familiar with Bernice's mania for cooking. She fries and roasts and bakes obsessively, but doesn't ever eat her own meals, preferring KFC instead, or furtive spoonfuls of Kraft Dinner late at night from a Tupperware container in the fridge. She cooks for social status, and of course she cooked for Stan, to whom she related adoringly and almost exclusively through ham. After he died, to judge from the content of these freezers, she scrabbled like a gerbil on a wheel, still cooking with the same energy but to no purpose. Then suddenly she stopped. As I scanned the Tupperware labels, I noted that everything in the freezers dated back to last summer.

I didn't know what to make of this. I come from a background in which deep freezers are as alien as butter churns. Everyone in my extended family purchases just enough groceries to last two days, and anything assigned to Tupperware—which, in my mother's case, tends to be a single cooked carrot—invariably perishes from neglect at the back of the fridge.

I think of it as a fusion of Scots frugality—in which an abundance of provisions is somehow considered unseemly—with that weird, upper-middle-class cuisine aesthetic you find in certain restaurants, where you order filet mignon, and it arrives wobbling atop a little dollop of whipped potatoes, and the rest of the huge white plate is scattered decoratively with parsley minced so fine that the only way you could actually consume it would be to pick up the plate and lick it off. When Calvin and I go for dinner at my uncle's house, Calvin has learned to consume a cheeseburger first, because he knows that there will not be a sufficient meal. "Calvin," my aunt Rose will say, ladling one tablespoonful of beef stroganoff onto a Royal Doulton china plate destined for Calvin's end of the table, "the asparagus is wonderfully fresh right now, will you have a stalk?"

In my experience, WASPs derive the bulk of their calories from scotch and cashews, neither of which are much prized in Cape Breton.

Lester and I decided to set up a Christmas crèche on the dining room table. I wanted to teach him the Christmas story, now that he knew about Heaven. I was a lapsed and untutored Christian, true, but still I found it discomfiting that my son understood Christmas to be an exceptionally lucky day, upon which ten new model dinosaurs from the Carnegie Museum collection arrived in bright packages, along with a sock full of sweets, plus Granny and turkey, all for no apparent reason.

Now, in Bernice's house, I felt a certain childlike delight in laying out the figurines for her crèche. I began to remember my mother's little display on the credenza in our Toronto house when I was young, which she laid out over a great spread of green felt. She stacked *The Art of Mexico* and other coffee-table books beneath the felt to create a topography, placing the manger triumphantly atop a plateau created by *Ontario Summer Cottages*. My mother's crèche was a colorful, mismatched array of figures: a tiny holy family she had purchased in France, some sandalwood camels from India that got knocked over by the mere breeze of someone passing by, a collection of Masai herdsmen made of ebony leading their cows, some hand-painted polka-dot chickens, and three oversized, papier mâché kings who stomped toward the manger like a trio of Godzillas and threatened to squash its inhabitants. I used to snitch Jesus, as I recall, and offer him as an adoptive son for Barbie until my mother took stock on Christmas Eve and invariably demanded him back.

Bernice's crèche was much more harmonious. Everyone in it was Bavarian. She had imported all the figurines from a German company that specialized in nativity scenes. Lester and I unwrapped them from their clumps of tissue paper and prepared to re-create the holy night when all was calm and all was bright. And silent, like at the end of *Goodnight Moon*. Goodnight stars, goodnight air, goodnight noises everywhere. I unwrapped a pair of bearded, white-robed men in sandals, and had no idea who they were.

"So these men," I murmured to my son, flipping them over to read their labels, "are the *Jünger, die Christus bewachen.*"

"The what?" asked Lester.

"Never mind."

"Donkeys!" he exclaimed, letting two or three miniature beasts of burden tumble to the table from their tissue wrappings. He scrambled off his chair and ran to find his allosaurus, whose new job was to menace the donkeys, and then at some point engage in a highly eccentric conversation with them. I unwrapped a fourth donkey that had a blue-gowned woman seated side-saddle on its back. "Ah!" I said, consulting the chart. "*Die Herbergsuche!*" Ambivalent, I placed her beside a little clump of bushes on the outskirts of the scene, making a note to myself to move her closer to the action if it turned out she was important.

Eventually the jackpot: *die Heilige Familie.* I set them up in the manger, with baby Jesus in an oval-shaped bed of painted clay straw. By now, all the donkeys and sheep had been cornered by large, predatory dinosaurs and were part of a hitherto-unknown subplot in the Christmas story involving livestock slaughter and a time warp. I found the three Wise Men, and arranged them in a humble queue that faced toward the manger. I salted in a coterie of angels.

"Okay, Lester, pay attention," I said. He came over from his end of the table for a closer look. "See this mommy and daddy and baby, here? This is why we celebrate Christmas, because it's baby Jesus's birthday. This is Jesus, and these are his parents, Mary and Joseph."

Lester studied the manger scene. "Why did his mommy name him after a swear word?"

"Well, no," I said, laughing, "the whole reason that Daddy shouldn't say 'Jesus H. Christ' when he's driving—you know how he says that?—is because that's taking . . . that's saying Jesus's name in a bad mood." I held up the baby Jesus and waggled him gently. "And we're only supposed to say 'Jesus' when we're happy. Yay Jesus, halleluja, that sort of thing."

"Is Santa going to bring him a present?" he asked.

"These three Wise Men do." I tapped each of them on the head. "They each have a present for him."

"What are Wise Men?"

I thought about this, and realized that I could not say why they were called that, exactly. "They're smart people," I proposed. "Wise is another word for smart. They were wise because they knew that Jesus was born, and that he was very important."

"Are they giving him toys?"

I gestured helplessly. "You know what? They're not giving him toys, actually, they're giving him"—no point reading the labels—"frankincense and myrrh . . . which are . . . which are . . . I think one of them was a smokable perfume? kind of thing, and the other one was, like, an herb."

Lester's eyes widened as if I were completely mad. "Why don't they give him a car?"

"No, look, the point is that when baby Jesus was born, that was the first Christmas, his birthday, because he was the son of God, and the Wise Men knew that . . . somehow . . . and that's why they showed up, and those were the kinds of presents available then. They hadn't invented plastic, yet, or toy stores." I leaned forward and brushed cracker crumbs from his chin. "Jesus was the one who first told us all about Heaven—you know how Granny was telling you about Heaven?" Of course, that wasn't right, what with Abraham and Moses and so on, but it would do.

"How could baby Jesus talk?" Lester asked, skeptical.

"Well, when he got older."

He stabbed his finger at the figure of Joseph. "Is that God?"

I sat back and scrubbed at my face with my hands.

"No, that's Joseph, who was cuckolded by a dove. I don't know where God is."

"What's cuck—"

"Never mind."

Lester generally knew when he'd come to the end of Twenty Questions with me and it was time to back off. He returned to the business of massacring sheep at the other end of the table. "Can I have some juice?"

I got up and padded into the kitchen. The radio on Bernice's blond vinyl counter was playing "Santa Baby," and outside, I could hear the crunch of a fender-bender on King Street, the sound of honking horns muffled by the thickly falling snow. I cracked open the fridge and reached for a bottle of Sunny Delight. "Santa Baby, slip a sable under the tree for me . . ."

Lester followed me, in his restless, zigzaggy fashion, and climbed onto the counter to drink his juice, banging his feet back and forth against the cupboards beneath.

"Momma," he asked, changing the subject to something he hoped wouldn't frustrate me, "if you spat on a plant, would it grow?"

8

"Oh, Lord in Heaven!"

We had just come off the elevator with a bag of apples and some coffee, and we could hear Bernice's wail clear down the corridor.

I broke into a run, slamming my hand over the lid of my coffee cup to keep it from spilling, Lester trotting behind in his ungainly snowsuit. We reached the threshold of Room 12 and found four helpless women crying out in unison, with Bernice on the floor beside her bed, and the others trapped by their various casts and IVs, unable to assist her. Bernice's nightie was twisted around her stomach, and she had her knees up and was scuffling at the floor in her sock feet like an enormous overturned turtle.

"Granny!" Lester exclaimed, "why are you wearing a diaper?"

"Shhh!" I waved him back. "Bernice," I asked, kneeling down, "what happened?"

"I tried to get out of bed to go to the bathroom and—oh!—I fell, and I've smashed my head! Jesus take my soul."

She moaned, eliciting murmurs of sympathy from her bedridden roommates, and an absolutely stricken look from Lester.

"I won't let him take your soul, Granny, I won't let him," Lester vowed, beginning to cry. I don't know what he thought a soul was, exactly, but he stood there uncertainly, on guard, with his little fists bunched to show his bravery as the snow melted and puddled around his boots. I picked him up, nuzzled his ear and placed him gently on Celia's bed, tugging off his boots while Celia unzipped his jacket.

"You're not going to die, Bernice," I said, returning to her and smoothing her hair. "It's just a matter of getting back into bed." I set down my coffee, leaned forward and felt gingerly behind her thin curls. She wasn't bleeding, and didn't have what I imagined would feel like a fracture. "You're fine," I assured her, and I slipped my arm beneath her rounded back, trying to pull her to a sitting position. She was so lax and uncooperative that it was like trying to manhandle a mattress.

"It ain't no use," she grumbled, "this old carcass can't be moved no more, I'm just a bag of bones."

"It's okay," I murmured.

"Are you going to float to Heaven now?" Lester asked, saucer-eyed, as I pulled her onto her bed.

"Oh no, dear," Bernice said, drawing the blanket up around her, "but I certainly don't mind that idea of floating. Just look at me, all swollen up. My soul's going to say good riddance to this wreck of a body, I'll tell you that."

"But isn't your *body* going with you?" Lester looked deeply confounded. Celia pulled him onto her lap and gave him a squeeze while I tended to Bernice. "We don't take these bodies with us to Heaven," she told him lightly. "We get to turn into beautiful angels with lovely white wings."

Needless to say, I was made to elaborate on this astounding new concept an hour later, as we headed to the Mayflower Mall for some Christmas shopping. "Sooner or later, animals die and humans die," I ventured, in reply to his queries from the back seat. "But what that means is that we change, like caterpillars turning into butterflies, only we turn into . . ." Well, there's a debate for you. But Celia had answered him; I could go with the flow. *We turn into angels.*

I glanced in the rearview mirror and noticed that Lester was craning his head to see the sky, looking totally perplexed. "But *where?*" he asked.

As it turned out, there were angels galore at the Mayflower Mall. Blond, for the most part. Hanging from the ceiling, or singing in the windows of the shops. In the toy store, we found angels alongside dinosaurs, who in turn shared shelf space with robots and dragons. All equally plausible, I suppose, from Lester's point of view.

In the autumn, Calvin and I had taken him to the Royal Ontario Museum and stumbled across a temporary exhibit on loan from the Museum of Anthropology in Mexico City. It was all about Aztec culture, complete with a display of sacrificed human remains.

"Daddy, what are those?" Lester had wanted to know, his nose pressed against the smudged glass of the exhibit.

"Skeletons, buddy," Calvin had answered.

"Dinosaur skeletons?"

"No. Human."

"But," I'd added, worried that Calvin was being too brusque, "humans who died a very long time ago, Les. Ancient skeletons."

"Oh." Lester stared for a very long time, as Calvin and I perused the rest of the exhibit and sought our own small revelations.

"Momma," he said, as the three of us walked home, kicking contentedly through drifts of leaves, "tell me a story about dead humans."

Hmmm. "You know what? I don't think I know a story about dead humans." *As such.*

Calvin had chuckled. He loved the idea that Lester thought of dead humans as a separate species that would never include him. Dogs, elves, dinosaurs, humans and *dead* humans, like the "mysterious race of skeleton people" uncovered by archeologists, as reported in a satirical news article that I once read in *The Onion*. The archeologists debated whether or not the skeleton people engaged in agriculture, or some other economic system, since it was clear to all that any grain they ate would fall out through their ribs.

"Personally," I'd told Calvin later, "I want Lester to have this view of life indefinitely, where there are no beginnings and no endings, neither facts nor fictions, just a whole, wondrous marvel of creatures side by side."

"Good luck," Calvin had said. I could tell he'd been thinking about Stan by the way his cynicism was darker than usual. "Life just has a way of forcing the truth."

9

"Is Santa Jesus's uncle?" Lester asked while we scanned the shelves at New Waterford's video store in search of a Christmas film that didn't star Tim Allen. "I guess so. Sort of." The extroverted, gift-plying uncle that undermines parental authority and makes God compete for our favors.

"Can we get this?" He pointed to an empty video box for *Frosty the Snowman*.

"Sure, sweetie." I took the box over to Cindy, the teenager who always seemed to work here, her chin in her hands with her elbows on the counter as she stared at a small TV.

"How's Bernice doin'?" Cindy asked as she handed me my change.

"Pretty good today," I answered. I was beginning to sound like Barbara.

My son threw snowballs as we trudged back to the house, and then asked me why Santa didn't bring presents for grown-ups.

"He's given up on us," I said. Then I glanced at Lester, worried that I sounded as despondent as I felt. "I'm just kidding. He has his hands full with you kids, that's all."

Lester spied an icicle and attempted to dislodge it while I wondered how long it would be before his curiosity about everything in the universe led him to the truth about Santa. When I was eight, as I recall, it dawned on me for the very first time that the prospect of one fat man entering and exiting several million chimneys around the globe within a span of twenty-four hours was unlikely, and I asked my mother to review the logistics. She declined, but upon further interrogation she conceded that Santa Claus was "somewhat mythical," and that she had felt it best that I come to that conclusion on my own. Having admitted as much, she settled back into her armchair and resumed reading *My Mother, My Self* by Nancy Friday.

I vividly remember standing ramrod straight and trying to bite back a sudden flow of tears. "LIAR!" I burst out. "You *lied* to me!"

"Oh, for heaven's sake," my mother responded dryly, "Santa Claus is a wonderful Christmas tradition, and it didn't do you any harm to think your stocking was from him, and not from me."

My mother was a psychologist. Everything was relative, in her view. She practiced Christian rituals with a similar indifference as to whether they were rooted in truth. She even sang me the classic nursery song "Jesus loves me, this I know." And look what else she claimed to know, the liar. When Santa imploded, right away it raised the dubious authenticity of God. I didn't want that to happen to Lester. He was showing me something that I had forgotten about myself: a natural capacity for reverence.

My son believed in Santa, and that was entirely his parents' doing, albeit with some assistance from multiple viewings of *Rudolph the Red-Nosed Reindeer*, *Frosty the Snowman* and numerous seasonal commercials, billboards and lawn ornaments. But where was he going? He was being led toward betrayal. Was that recommended by Dr. Spock? And what would he do when he got there? Santa would take Jesus down with him.

"You know what?" I said, as we reached the carport Stan had built to house the car he rarely drove. "It's still early, maybe we could go to church. They might have a Christmas pageant, which is a play that tells the story of Jesus and the Wise Men. Do you want to do that?"

"Okay," he said, always up for an excursion.

Sunday was a beautiful day for a drive. Provided that we stayed in our rental car with the heat cranked up and ten hats on our heads, and peered at the scenery through the breath-dampened slit beneath hats and above scarves as I attempted to drive without the benefit of flexible arms. The snow was smooth and glassy, and the ocean deceptively bright—although we weren't far from where the *Titanic* foundered. This ocean chilled bones in April.

Ahead of us on a snowy rise was St. James Anglican Church, of pristine clapboard and straight, slender steeple. I do love all the Anglican churches I attended at Christmas in childhood, so wonderfully lit with glimmering candles, and redolent with the scents of wool and snow and incense. I felt sweetened by this vision of St. James, and after we parked, I led Lester into the vestibule for his first-ever church service.

The air was warm and thick inside. The organ murmured as parishioners tilted heads one to the other and whispered their gossip and recipes. The church's interior was unpainted, built of honey-colored cedar, which warmed the pale winter light streaming in through the windows. Beyond the wreath-laden altar, and the wooden crucifix of Christ in his dying moments, a stained-glass window faced the ocean. It was a lovely church, a wonderful place for God. Lester suddenly stopped dead beside me, exclaiming in high alarm: "What happened to *that* guy?" He was pointing at the crucifix. I hushed him, but then started laughing, and as we took our seats in a pew, I grew deeply worried that I wouldn't be able to stop. It would be like attending chapel during my years at school, when we were made to stand up and sit down and stand up and sit down and then drone a hymn in unison, "Holy, Holy, Holy, Lord God Almighty," about as melodiously as accountants on quaaludes. Me and my friend Mary Ann would start giggling until we thought we might burst.

Here I was, introducing my son to the House of the Lord as I pissed myself laughing. I squirmed and gritted my teeth and lectured myself with icy sternness: How dare you succumb to hysterics in a church service, at your age.

"Momma, what's so funny?" asked Lester without moderating his voice, even as the hawk-nosed priest intoned, "Let us pray." Two elderly ladies behind us smiled at Lester, more taken with his innocence than they were dismayed with me. How could I thank them? At last I was able to vent my hilarity by joining the congregation in belting out "Joy to the World," as boisterous as Ethel Merman.

When it came time for Communion, I took Lester's hand and we made our way to the altar, inching up the aisle in blank, obedient silence. We reached the velvet-cushioned pew and I sank to my knees, head bowed reverently with my hands clasped like a schoolgirl. When the deacon came to me and held forth the chalice, I leaned forward to have a sip, but it was nearly empty and he wasn't holding it at a sufficient tilt, so that I sipped air fruitlessly from its rim. I jutted my head forward and tried to slurp, which provoked a deeply offended stare. The deacon indicated that I was supposed to tip the chalice myself, instead of keeping my hands clutched piously at my waist. The Communion wafer was a smoother affair, thank God; I didn't have to snap at it like Pac-Man. The deacon and his assistant glided past me, and also past Lester, who burst out in dismay: "Why don't I get a chip?"

On the way out, I saw a note in the vestibule advertising the pageant for next week. I wasn't sure I had the nerve to return.

*   *   *

Driving back to Bernice's, I wondered anew at my stunningly poor religious education. When I looked back at those Sundays when I attended the High Anglican services at holidays, it seemed to me that the trouble always lay in the language, which was so stiff and archaic that it lost me. Sermons delivered without charisma, the congregation incapable of emoting or moving a muscle to the music—most of the services I went to were as insufferably dull as after-school detentions. This was curious, in a way, because the church was actually founded in the fervent pursuit of sexual passion by Henry VIII, who broke from Rome in order to dump Queen Catherine of Aragon so he could caress Anne Boleyn's "duckies," which were being withheld from him. Yet Henry's Church of England, forged in the exalted spirit of desire, went on to become such a stodgy dowager that modern Catholicism looks positively histrionic by comparison.

I will fall over and die the day that I see an Anglican parishioner slapping her thighs, swaying, clapping and bellowing "halleluja" in the presence of the Lord, instead of staring stone-faced at the backs of other people's hats. It's no longer about God, as far as I can tell. It's about decorum.

If one belongs to the Church of England, one bakes biscuits for the after-service social in the parish hall. Not too many biscuits, however, for one does not wish to appear vain and bountiful.

One is never bountiful, and certainly never ecstatic. One does not get knocked off one's horse, like Paul on the road to Damascus, for one could not abide such wild and discomposing surrender—the equivalent of making a sound during orgasm.

How does one find God, once one has lost Him, in all the distracting busy work of making biscuits and writing books of etiquette, one might ask?

One does not know.

10

On Monday, I had a glorious epiphany. After twenty years of drinking takeout coffee, it suddenly occurred to me that the little square dent in the middle of the cup lid was put there to hold down the plastic flap, so that it doesn't slap against your lip when you drink.

I announced my discovery to Calvin during our evening phone call, and he reminded me that it took me two years to realize that I could skip messages on my call-answer service by pressing the number six.

"Not that that's important," he added. "Congratulations on your new relationship to coffee-cup lids, Frannie, but you'd be better off knowing how to start a fire with twigs."

Calvin ought to know, of course. He has started approximately no fires, ever, with twigs, or anything else, not even matches. The only thing he lights is his hash pipe. Still, he merely warms to concepts of self-sufficiency, inasmuch as his world-view distills into something like this: The world is gonna end. We'll blow ourselves up and germs'll take over; good riddance to humans. This is Calvin's version of clarity. He gets it from his father. Anybody who survives Armageddon will subsist on a diet of rodents, and if they don't know how to hunt rats with pointed sticks, they can shove their Palm Pilots up their asses and beg for mercy.

Now and then, I press Calvin to elaborate on this vision, or at least on its psychological origins, and he argues that he is not a gloom-ridden misanthrope, not at all, but that it is hubris for anyone to believe that technology improves our lives in a meaningful way. In the end, he says, it cannot save us from ourselves.

The most important technology in Calvin's life at the moment is the kitchen blender, upon which he has recently learned how to play "A Bicycle Built for Two."

11

Here are some of the important technologies in my life, and I can't help noting, as I jot them down, that the majority have yet to be invented:

A TV that automatically turns on at seven every morning, and shows three back-to-back episodes of Franklin the Turtle.

A breakfast robot—other than myself—that can dispense toasted English muffins with peanut butter on a plastic Ikea plate to small children watching Franklin *on TV.*

A genetically engineered money tree.

Laser-guided eyeballs for the back of my head.

BELIEVE ME

A remote that can put other people on mute.

A radar device that can track the flight of angels.

On Tuesday, technology confounded me again. It was teatime at the Regional. In a hospital, teatime generally means supper time, because everyone keeps farmers' hours for no apparent reason. Bernice and I were discussing the foodstuffs on her tray.

"Dr. Richardson said to put the medicine in my ginger ale?" she asked, her expression a wondrous mingling of horror, skepticism and disgust, as if I'd just advised her that she'd swallowed a grub.

"He just suggested it," I reassured her. "He thought you'd be happier about taking it if you dissolved it first in a drink." I squeezed her hand, which was papery and cool.

"It's a cancer medicine, isn't it?" she demanded to know.

I shook my head. "I really don't think so, Bernice, I think it's for indigestion."

Her expression grew pensive. She rolled herself onto her side, away from where I sat on the chair. "These doctors don't know nothing," she muttered. "When I get home, I'm changing to that doctor in Sydney. The one Shirley had last year. Get him to switch my asthma medicine and take me off all them other pills."

I dipped my head down. Felt my chest tighten. Did Bernice need to arrive at some sort of reckoning about her predicament? I tilted a can of strawberry Ensure into her glass, and then sat quietly for a few minutes. To judge from the rise and fall of her shoulders, she was falling asleep.

"Do you want to have a nap now?" I asked softly.

She nodded weakly. I got up to reach for her mask. I had initially thought it was an oxygen mask, but Celia explained that it misted some sort of respiratory medication that Bernice needed to inhale before sleeping. A jumbo dose of Dristan, or something. I pulled the mask off its hook, and wondered if it hadn't gotten a bit smudged and dirty in the last few days, going on and off her face with no one cleaning it. So I breathed into it— "haaa"—and wiped it with my sleeve, the way you do when you're cleaning your sunglasses, and was just thinking that I really shouldn't have done that, when the neon lights blinked out overhead. All at once the room was lit only by the pallor of a winter afternoon, which felt simultaneously more natural and somewhat alarming.

"Good heavens," said Aileen, who had been listening to the radio. "My music stopped and now my fan isn't whirring."

A most interesting coincidence.

"It's the power," murmured Celia, who was sitting cross-legged in her bed with one hand massaging her back, and the other lightly on Lester, to whom she had been reading *Poppleton in Spring*. She was sweating profusely. "My morphine drip has cut out."

"*Good heavens,*" Aileen said again, but now she was staring at Julia's corner of the room.

Julia's special air mattress was slowly deflating. The

electric pump that regulated its pressure had stopped. She was sinking, fast asleep, between the metal bed rails, like a noblewoman on a funereal Viking boat drifting out to sea. We all gaped, open-mouthed.

"You'd better do something, Frannie," Aileen said.

I dutifully rushed over to Julia's bed without being able to formulate the slightest inkling of what the something was that I should do. "Julia! Wake up!" I urged softly as I clutched her bed rails. It turns out that a deeply slumbering and arthritic ninety-three-year-old is slower to leap into action than you might hope. I tried to cushion her slow-motion descent, as she perilously closed in on the bed's metal underpinnings, by . . . oh . . . hmmm. I yanked Bernice's pillow from under her tousled head— which went thwack against her mattress—and began trying to push it under Julia's back.

Aileen struggled to get up and help me, throwing her arm out with such haste that she knocked over her fan, whereupon the power surged back on, Julia suddenly reversed course and began to ascend, and a large number of Hostess potato chips flew across the room like a cloud of locusts, propelled by the overturned fan. Lester shouted in delight and reached out to catch them. Celia curled forward, head to knees, collapsing in laughter, and Aileen joined in, covering her mouth with the back of one hand and looking mischievous, as if she'd played a deliberate prank. Bernice, on the other hand, flailed at the chips and began to wheeze.

"Oh dear," I said, trotting to her side. "I'm so sorry." I fumbled with her mask as she gasped for air, bug-eyed.

But I couldn't make out which button to push to start misting her, and came close to tears at my own stupidity. When I finally had her settled, I went and stood in the hallway, bereft.

Dr. Richardson was approaching with his arms behind his back, and this time, I was the one who ran away.

I am comforted by sunlight, like a cat. I basked in it the next morning, as I sat by the tall, bright windows of the hospital meeting room, face tilted upward, hands behind my head, waiting for Father McPhee. The light was so serene and the room so neutral that I felt briefly out of time, the way one feels on an airplane when the sun has just risen above the feathery bed of clouds outside the window, radiant, and there's nothing to anticipate but coffee and a square of scrambled eggs.

"You wanted to see me?"

Father McPhee barged into my solitude. I opened my eyes to greet him, and saw that he was enormously fat, mostly about the middle. He was shaped rather like a top. He whirled in, grabbed a chair, swung it around and plunked himself down, knees apart, directly in front of me, chair to chair at the window. He had a huge grin on his face.

"You're Frances, Bernice's daughter-in-law," he announced, slapping me on the leg. His movements were expansive and cocky. This jarred me. For some reason, I thought Bernice's beloved "Faa'ther McPhee" would be a member of her own generation, morose and outdated, a fading apparition of piety. But no, this guy looked as if he were barely pushing forty, with trim, receding chestnut hair, a pointy nose and sharp little eyes that glinted through rectangular spectacles.

"Yes," I said. "That's right. Or, at least, I'm with her son Calvin. I don't know if you know him."

"The orchestra player," he replied, his expression brightening back into a grin. "Bernice wouldn't know the difference between Sid Vicious and Mahler, is that fair to say?" He winked.

I stared at him in surprise. "You know that Calvin doesn't play in an orchestra?"

"Oh, sure, sure." He kept grinning. I waited for him to elaborate, but he didn't. I suppose he and Calvin met when Stan died. To arrange the funeral. It quickly became evident that Father McPhee was expansive with his physical presence, but not with his words. He kept staring at me. Kept grinning, his hands clasped between his knees. I cleared my throat.

"Right. Well, anyway, thank you for meeting with me, I appreciate it because I wondered if I could have your advice."

"Oh, sure."

"I need to talk to Bernice about her health."

"What health?" He winked.

I smiled, har har, and looked down at my hands. "Well, exactly, that's the problem. Her cancer has come out of remission and the chickens are, as some might say, coming home to roost."

"Sounds like you've been talking to Dr. Richardson." He winked again.

"Well, yes, so I don't know the specifics, but I have to assume that she's close to dying—I mean, I guess that's what Dr. Richardson means—and I feel this is something she should be discussing with people who love her."

"Oh sure." He was jiggling one fat knee up and down. Too much coffee?

I wondered—what should I call him? Father or Your Honor? I wasn't sure and it seemed important. Doctor, doctor, what do I do?

"The thing is, um, sir," I cringed, "it's difficult to talk to Bernice about the situation in medical terms." I frowned, trying to think of the right words. "Or even, you know, even existentially or spiritually, or . . ." I tilted my head back and breathed in deeply, fiddled with an earring. "Am I making any sense? I feel like I should be reading her some Dylan Thomas poetry—you know that famous poem 'Do Not Go Gentle into That Good Night'? Although, of course, Thomas wound up dying by falling drunk off a barstool, so I can't say he set the most inspiring example himself, maybe that's not a good idea, but there's a wonderful poem by Walt Whitman I could read her, this beautiful section of *Leaves of Grass*."

He nodded in recognition, but said nothing.

"But then I can't," I went on. "For one thing, what Whitman is talking about is totally posthumous, and that's weird, and kind of mean, and then if I ever bring up any kind of prospect of reckoning, it would be like triggering a smoke alarm. I'm worried she'll shriek with terror." At that, I faltered, and smiled apologetically.

"Sure, that's Bernice," he said, still grinning. Was this funny? I opened my mouth, then clapped it shut. I suddenly worried about what I was doing, in the Good Father's mind. I was gossiping, maybe. Perhaps he had no intention of advising me at all. I swallowed hard.

Father McPhee at last rid himself of his grin and straightened, pushing at his glasses, coughing, and gazing downward as he assembled his thoughts.

"Frances," he ventured, "my experience, such as it is, and maybe I'm not old, but I'm certainly *around* the old, is that people die the way they live." He held my gaze. "Bernice has not lived her life reflectively and searchingly, is that fair to say?"

I nodded and bit my upper lip, suddenly on the verge of tears. How would I know if she's lived her life searchingly? I've only met the woman *three times.*

"In some ways," he continued, "Bernice is more like a child than an old woman. Which is—you know, the elderly often become childlike because they lose their faculties, they grow dependant—but Bernice has always been like that. Since I've known her. Like a particularly upsettable child. I don't why that is, Frances." He paused, in case I wished to provide an explanation, which I could not. "But I do know that she will not change on her deathbed. In most cases—God will correct me if I'm wrong—people just keep on living, keep on complaining or joking or raging or drinking, you know, whatever, until they fall off their barstools. Even when they're administered their last rites, they are still very much animated by what drove them all along. With Stan, your father-in-law, I came in—I don't know if Calvin told you this—I came in when he was in the Regional with pneumonia a couple of years ago; we thought he was very close. And the nurse explained why I was there, and he said: 'I ain't seein' no priest on my deathbed. This is a special occasion, and I ain't gonna talk to no one but the Pope.'" He laughed at the memory, his sides shaking, then sobered and leaned toward me. "Nor *should* you feel obliged to change her."

I wasn't about to argue. I sat there still as stone, considering the truth of what he'd said.

"On the other hand, Bernice has always been very open to receiving God. As I recall, she is very devoted to St. Anne de Beaupré. I believe that's her patron saint?"

I nodded. I'd seen several St. Anne knickknacks in the house. Curious, I looked her up on the Internet and found out she was the patron saint of broommakers, French-Canadian fur traders, housewives and lost articles.

"So the great task," McPhee concluded, crossing his hamlike arms, "of bringing the soul closer to God, has already been accomplished. Do you see this? All that is left for you to do, Frances, is to call upon God with your own prayers."

"What do you mean?" I bit my thumbnail. Was God going to take care of this and let me get back to my own life?

"Pray for Bernice. Support her soul's journey toward death and onward to Heaven through prayer."

"Oh." I winced at my childishness.

BELIEVE ME

The priest cocked his chin to one side and considered me, clearly attuned to such instantaneous Good Person/ Bad Person struggles within his parishioners. "Is there anything you would like to confess?"

"I beg your pardon?"

"The words spoken in confession are guarded by the most solemn obligation of confidentiality, and I certainly hold that to be true in all circumstances. Is there anything you'd like to confess to, Frances?"

"Oh . . . that's very nice of you." Did he know I wasn't Catholic? I was caught between confessing that I didn't understand what he meant, and confessing anything else. "You mean, right now? Today's sins?"

"Whatever is troubling your conscience."

My shoulders drooped and I sighed. I thought about Bernice's kitchen stuff. The greed tic. How I'd lied about something to Avery in November. How I dumped that guy in high school. And then, for some reason, I remembered that jet-lagged morning in Spain, long ago, in the house my mother rented in Malaga, when I accidentally went number two in a bidet. In a panic of embarrassment, I denied all responsibility when my mother found something wrapped in paper, sprayed with perfume, and concealed in the wastebasket. I suggested that she ask my grandmother. Rank exploitation of the elderly was emerging as a theme. I remembered other things too, worse things I'd done, which flashed into my conscious mind and disappeared into the dark of denial as swiftly as heat lightning. If, by your late thirties, you

82

haven't gone to confession, it's more like Life Review on Judgment Day than a quick Hail Mary.

"Nothing important," I mumbled.

"Everything is important in God's eyes."

"Well, I can't see that." I raised my head to argue, "I imagine someone confessing to strangling eleven old ladies with a nylon is going to have a more important conversation with God than someone who wants her dying mother-in-law's wok."

"You are covetous, then."

"Only of appliances."

"Go on."

I felt like kicking myself for giving him something to work with. "It's not like I want to go out and buy appliances. I do not covet *all* appliances. It's just that I don't have very many, and Bernice has tons, which are all just sitting around her house unused. Really, some of them are still in their boxes. And I wouldn't even bring it up, except that I feel guilty about the fact that I'm thinking of Bernice's stuff this way. But I can't help it, because . . . the truth is, I don't like her. I don't like Bernice, and I want her wok."

I was aflame with a sense of my own ridiculousness at this point, and couldn't meet Father McPhee's eyes. He said nothing for a moment, and then I felt his palm resting lightly on my knee.

I looked up, tentative. "So?"

"So?" he echoed, amused.

"So, what should I do?"

He resumed his original posture, elbows on his knees, eyes glinting behind the glasses, that big fat grin. "Don't pine for woks, Frances. Set them aside. Give them away. Take Bernice herself up into your arms and pray for the Lord's guidance."

I nodded, rubbing my eyes, playing an imaginary game of Whack-A-Mole with the disgruntled and irritable thoughts that kept popping up in my mind, chief among them, "Damn it all to hell."

"I know what you're thinking," McPhee said.

Oh, God, I hope not.

"You're thinking you can't do it. But I'll tell you something: I may be a Catholic, but I'm not so narrow-minded I can't quote a Jewish rabbi. Do you know Rabbi Herschel?"

"No," I shook my head.

"That's okay. You don't need to know who he was, just what he said. He said—and I've always liked this—'Religion begins with a consciousness that something is asked of us.'"

12

Christmas Eve. Santa Claus was coming, and so was Bernice. I'd hummed an anxious little song about it that morning, as I'd rushed around the house trying to make everything look just so, recovering Bernice's medical gadgets and restoring some of her things.

"Can't see my chuckwagon," she announced right off the bat, as Calvin gingerly settled her into her easy chair by the fire. He himself had arrived only a few hours earlier, checked her out of the Regional and had yet to ease off his overcoat. Did Bernice think she couldn't see the chuckwagon because I had put a tree up, all twinkly and bright with nightgowns wrapped for her beneath, or was she making a broader comment about my rearrangements in the house?

"Momma hid it," Lester offered, from his perch on the arm of the couch. "She said it was a *thing.*"

"Okay, what he means by that," I hastened to add, tucking a blanket around her, "is that I didn't want him playing with your things."

Bernice made no reply. She was staring over the fireplace. "Is that a statue of Satan you put on my mantelpiece, Nancy, beside the Christmas carol trio, or what is that?"

"Oh. No, that's a pliosaur, actually," I said, as my cheeks flared crimson. "It's uh . . . it's one of Lester's prehistoric marine reptiles. He just—you know, he puts these things everywhere and I just lose track." Calvin chuckled, patting my back. He headed for the kitchen, saying over his shoulder, "Wanna cuppa tea, Mum?"

Bernice nodded weakly and Lester homed in on this new species, Satan.

"What's a Satan, Granny?" he asked, pulling lightly on her fingers, which hung limply off the edge of the armrest.

"Oh, don't worry about him, darlin'," Bernice said, still distracted by her own dismay, "he's just a fallen angel. The devil. You don't want him to know you, dear. No, not at all."

"Why?" Lester persisted. "Is he dangerous? Is he a meat-eater or a plant-eater?"

Bernice leaned her head on her chair back and laughed. Took off her glasses and rubbed her eyes. "Good Lord in Heaven, Lester, I don't know *what* the devil eats. But he takes souls. You just be good, don't listen to his voice, and he won't take yours."

*　　*　　*

Later, Calvin took Lester out to toboggan, and I found Bernice silently weeping in her chair. Was it the absence of Stan, I wondered, or the perturbation of pliosaurs and missing chuckwagons? Did she feel that her life was being dismantled and replaced? I can only imagine how distressing that sense of displacement would be. I hovered.

"Oh, go on," she said, waving me away, "you go on and fix up Lester's presents. I'm just tired, that's all."

It was unclear to me what Bernice noticed, or didn't notice about her house, and I found myself compulsively worrying over each small transgression. Did she register that Lester and I had eaten all of her toffees? Was that okay, since we were guests? Or had we been hogs? Had she seen that I'd opened and investigated a box containing a brand-new pressure cooker? Just looked. I put it back beside the box of knives. Did she think I wanted to steal it?

Certainly, she seemed to think that Dana had pinched a knobby orange throw rug that no longer sat folded on the bureau beside her bed, and since neither Calvin nor I could locate this rug, after an earnest and irrationally guilt-ridden search, we had to agree that it had somehow exited the house. Later, we would learn that Bernice had sold it at a yard sale but forgotten. This wound up accounting for the lawn mower, too, and a number of other objects she'd been complaining about all autumn. But we hadn't been around to monitor the humdrum transactions of her life. We had no idea what was true.

We were lost with her, self-conscious and under suspicion, in the fun house of her own forgetfulness.

"No need to buy a turkey, Nancy," Bernice had told me at the hospital, when I said I was headed to the IGA for Christmas dinner groceries. "Been savin' one in the freezer. Got cranberry sauce down there, too. Lots of it. The secret to good cranberry sauce is not too much sugar. Shirley always spoils it, makes it too sweet."

"Oh, okay," I answered, "that makes things easier. Will you eat potatoes, Bernice, if I buy some?"

"You go on and get what you want, dear, I'll eat what I can."

So I did, and then, surprise. I went down on Christmas Eve to pull out the turkey for thawing, and found nothing resembling fowl, not even a chicken, residing in those arctic boxes filled with soup and jam.

"Oh, Lord in Heaven!" Bernice exclaimed from her easy chair, when I broke the news. "Dana's stolen my turkey right out from under me!" She tugged at her white tufts of hair in distress and held a balled fist to her mouth to keep from crying.

"I didn't take no turkey," Dana retorted with a snort of derision when I phoned her at home, at Bernice's insistence, to say, "Merry Christmas and where's the bird, you robber."

"Bernice don't even *cook* turkey for Christmas," Dana added. "Stan always wanted meat pie. You don't believe me, ask Shirley. Shirley brings over her turkey leftovers, sometimes, so's Bernice can make that rice soup she likes!"

"Alright," I said, trying to mollify Dana, "don't worry about it, I just promised Bernice that I'd ask. It's hard to tell what's true in what she says, you know."

"That's just because you ain't been around," Dana countered. "Otherwise it would be clear as the nose on your face."

"I know, and I'm sorry. It's confusing. Listen, have a Merry Christmas."

I hung up feeling desperate for a scotch. Lester and Calvin were in the kitchen, arranging a plate of Peek Freans to leave by the fire for Santa. "Are you sure Santa will know that we're here, and not home?" Lester pressed his father. "Are you *sure*?" He was very worried about it, as I had been the day before. ("Are you sure you remembered to buy Lester all the stuff I suggested. Are you *sure*?")

I brought Bernice another cup of tea and sat down across from her chair. When I relayed Dana's protestation of innocence, she rolled her head away from me, and closed her eyes. A tear began to wander down her withered cheek.

"It wouldn'a happened when Stan was alive, all this thieving and lying. Taking advantage of me."

A silence settled between us, and at length I reached for the remote and turned on the TV.

Calvin hated having Lester bear witness to his mother's fear.

"This is crap," he said, as we lay down on the pull-out couch in the living room and stared at the ruby lights of the tree. "You spend so much time convincing your child that the world is a safe place, you know?"

I knew.

"And then my mother blows it all to hell by announcing that in fact, *in fact*, the world is really out to kill you and rob you blind. Oh, and watch out for Satan. "

"She doesn't mean any harm," I said quietly, flinging one arm up over my head, exhausted from the last-minute blitz of present-wrapping and stocking-stuffing.

"Maybe we shouldn't have brought Lester here," Calvin said. His tone was bleak, belligerent. Characteristic of Cape Bretoners—fatalistic Scots and doomed Acadians who arrived in the new world desperate and fucked, and never got over it, just took refuge in their wonderful, mordant humor.

"We should have brought him home for Christmas," he continued. "We're freaking him out. I'll tell you what: I can't stand parenting at both ends—trying to keep one end from completely alarming the other."

"Well, it could be worse," I ventured, turning to press my nose into his flannel-shirted side, which smelled of deodorant and Christmas pine, and ever so faintly of scotch. "We could be living at any other time in history, when families stayed together until the bitter end, all the different generations in one hut, having to do everything, you know? Fart in front of one another. Make love. Die. The children saw all of that. And then the dead bodies would hang around in the parlor with flies on them for a while."

"Huts don't have parlors."

"Well, you know what I mean." I cuffed him lightly. "Like that time I spent those three months in Cuba, and there was a dead dog outside on the road one day, it must have been hit by a car. Did I ever tell you about this? So you think, oh that's grim and sad. The way you would think in Canada. But then it just stayed there. Nobody removed it. They didn't have a department of sanitation, or whatever, in that town. Plus, it was the dry season, it never rained, so the body took an extremely long time to decompose. So, eventually the sentiment shifts from 'Oh, that's grim and sad' to 'Hey, I wonder what state of decay that German shepherd is in today? Has the tongue fallen out of the skull yet?'"

Calvin raised himself up on his elbow and twisted around to stare at me in amusement. "And your point is?"

I sighed. Defensive. I rolled onto my other side. "It's not funny, Calvin. My point is that you can get used to anything. It's just how far removed you are from trying times that makes you worry about Lester. He's better off learning how to makes sense of the world now, for good and bad, than in expecting nothing to happen but sunshine and Santa."

"Oh, you *have* been thinking," Calvin murmured, sliding his arm around my waist and nosing into my neck. "I try not to do that on holidays."

We were still in bed the next morning, drugged with sleep, ruffled heads immovable beneath the floral quilt, when I heard Bernice and Lester chatting in the kitchen as Christmas dawned.

BELIEVE ME

I couldn't make out what she was saying—she spoke in such a rasping whisper these days—but I certainly caught my own boy's chipper Boy Scout sing-song. "It's okay, Granny," he told her, "you don't have to worry about the devil. He doesn't live in Canada."

13

Monday morning. Freezing rain. Hunkered down and glowering, I rode the crowded streetcar to work after a long month's absence, squished between two strangers talking on their cell phones. Bernice had returned to the Regional, unable to procure twenty-four-hour nursing until she'd been "signed over to palliative," as Dr. Richardson explained it, which nobody seemed prepared to do. So we flew home to resume our lives in the uncertain light of her illness.

"Hey, Jim. Whassup?" the man to the left of me suddenly barked. "Yeah, I'm on my way to the office. I did go skiing. Yeah. The powder was awesome." To my right, a young woman with blue-tinted hair sang out gaily, "*No way!* That is such a hoot! What do edible panties taste like?"

"Excuse me," I said, as the streetcar rolled sluggishly toward my stop. Engrossed as they were, neither of the strangers heard me. I thumped the woman lightly on the back, fueled by that momentary and ridiculous panic one feels that one will not successfully exit the vehicle. "I need to get past you, please."

"Do you mind?" she retorted, with startling indignation. "I'm *on the phone.*"

Several passengers, including me, stared at her for a beat and then laughed at the sheer witlessness of what she had said. I elbowed my way to the exit and stepped down onto the icy street in a much better mood.

Thankfully I did not dread returning to work, the way I used to when I held clerical jobs, just out of college. I used to sit at my desk completely mesmerized by the tick of the clock toward five. My pay hadn't improved much since those days, given that the *Review* couldn't attract high-end advertisers like Gucci, say, to flash wares between reviews of "Abortion: A Social History" and "The Bosnian Experience in Canada." But the work absorbed me and the space was quiet. In the renovated warehouse on Adelaide Street that held our modest office—a converted slaughterhouse with exposed-brick walls—Avery and I mostly sat in companionable silence.

Our loft was sparely furnished. Along one wall stood a slanted design table for Goran, our Croatian art director, who strolled in for a week or so at the end of each month to put the magazine to bed, otherwise devoting himself to designing Flash files for display on the Web.

We had a couple of rickety shelves for our books, and for us, two schoolteacher's desks that faced each other across a vast expanse of maple flooring. Manuscripts fanned out around each desk like plumage as we picked through the upcoming books we were going to assign for review. Avery and I consulted one another as if we were husband and wife dining at either end of a long, invisible table.

I told Avery about Lester's new acquaintance with religion, and he responded by quoting the comic Eddie Izzard, who he'd just seen performing at the Opera House, on the subject of how God made the world in seven days.

"On the first day he created light, and air, and fish, and jam, and soup, and potatoes, and haircuts, and arguments, and small things, and rabbits, and people with noses."

Avery spoke in a deep bass with crisp, scholarly pronunciation. If you were to hear him on the telephone, you might imagine a man of great physical presence and immaculate attire, an MI5 man perhaps, like James Bond's boss. But in fact he seemed rather tubercular, so slender his chest appeared to be concave. He wore dingy white dress shirts that billowed out at the front where his size-two pants were cinched with a belt, and more often than not, his shirt worked itself free and hung over his gray flannels like an apron. His chin was piquant, his cheeks sallow and his eyes enormous. He might have been beautiful, if he weren't so awkward.

Avery's looks had nothing to do with tragedy at Moulin Rouge and everything to do with the fact that he ate nothing but turkey. He was impossible to go to restaurants with, really, because he shunned almost all foodstuffs. If there wasn't turkey, which there rarely was, he would settle for minestrone soup with saltine crackers. Failing that, he would eat dinner rolls and sip ice water. Avery was the picky child whose mother had died when he was three, freezing him in the business of being picky; his father had never addressed his refusals and corrected them, and he'd grown to manhood with these peculiarities of diet, about which he was totally unselfconscious. Hand him a package of Maple Leaf turkey slices, and he would settle down as cheerfully as if he had a feast before him.

In spite of this malnutrition, he never lacked for energy. His arms were intriguingly elastic—they waved and twisted snakishly whenever he grew animated in conversation. Calvin had turned this unique display into a noun, which he called "Avery-ness." Nobody else waved their arms this way, or subsisted exclusively on Thanksgiving dinners, or revealed such a strange absence of awareness about all things twenty-first century. Avery wrote by hand, possessed neither a cell phone nor an answering machine, and didn't know how to drive. Instead, he pedaled around town on bicycles which were frequently stolen, because he tended to lock them to portable objects.

He was the sort of person to whom things happened, good or ill, entirely due to his Avery-ness. Once, for example, he got thrown out of the Drake Hotel, a chic bar very much consumed by its own image, because he hogged the bathroom for half an hour—by an oversight on Avery's part, it happened to be the women's bathroom—seated on the toilet reading the last chapter of his Pushkin novel, as if he were at home. He was unable to dispel the bartender's conviction that he had either barfed and passed out, or was in there snorting lines. I tried to rescue him to no avail, and he was summarily escorted out the door.

For all of his oddities, Avery was a man of great common sense and sly perceptiveness. Last year, he came up with the name for the new start-up magazine down the hall from us, when the editors were standing about scratching their heads and gnawing their pen tips.

"I have an idea," Avery had offered, not bothering to explain that his idea came straight out of a Mark Twain story about dueling, back-stabbing, gun-fighting broadsheet editors in the Confederate South. And the editors cried, "That's a great idea!" So it was that they unveiled Canada's first ultra-conservative magazine as the *Moral Volcano*.

It was a very important niche magazine, the *Moral Volcano*, for it swiftly became a must-read every week for the nation's conservatives. I had never met the proprietor, Frederick Dunst, but Avery's father had taught him Latin at private school, and thus Avery knew that Frederick was heir to the Dunst chocolate-peanut fortune. Further, Avery had heard that the younger Dunst once got three sheets to the wind with George W. Bush, at a party in Palm Beach in the mid-eighties. He developed such a nostalgic adoration for this magical night of slurred opinions, and held—at any rate—such similar views about homosexuals, Cubans and French politicians—that he eventually bankrolled a magazine to rally the Canadian right to the Bush cause. Naturally, he staffed it with like-minded thinkers, who I often ran into in the stairwell. We had this huffing, stair-climbing sort of passing acquaintance, in which we'd nod in recognition, but I didn't know anyone by name until I met Hilary. She was the managing editor, whose son Niall had been in kindergym with Lester.

"Why don't you come take a peek at our space," Hilary invited me one day after we ascended to the second floor together, chatting about how much preschoolers liked trampolines. Hilary was a moon-faced blond with wide-set green eyes and a penchant for wearing slimming black suits. Her husband, Brad, was a banker, she told me, which enabled her to afford monthly sprees at Holt Renfrew in spite of her editing salary. She had a big, robust laugh and a flair for hospitality.

Unlike our big empty rectangle of an office, the *Volcano* divvied up its half of the second floor into cubicles. There was a common lounge at the end, with an overstuffed leather couch and a coffee table piled with copies of the *Wall Street Journal* and the *National Review*. On the wall, someone had posted a large photograph of the United Nations, at which the editors threw suction-cup darts when they needed some downtime. "So that's a lot of fun," Hilary said. "And the other thing we do is, every Friday we break out the cocktails and destroy something French." She smiled and gave a mischievous wink.

Ah, so that explained it. I had wondered, once, when I was working late and walked down the hall to the bathroom, why the *Volcano* staff were chortling and hooting as they stomped on a baguette.

Hilary's description raised more questions than it answered, but I was too self-conscious to ask them. I didn't know how to bring it up as stairwell chat, because what I wanted to know, rather than being casual and jokey, would by necessity be pressing. "*What* is the deal with your hostility toward Gauls and multilateralism?" It was easier to confess all my sins to Father McPhee than to ask a loaded question like that.

14

This much I owed to Lester, and to Father McPhee. I would take my son to St. Stephen's, the little brick church down the street from us in Toronto, last refuge for a smattering of Anglicans in a community now dominated by Portuguese Catholics, Vietnamese Buddhists and Goths, so that Lester could wrap his mind around Heaven and Hell and I could kneel down on a pew with my parka bunched around my waist and think nice things about Bernice.

I suppose I might have chosen a different church, if I'd had the faintest clue how to shop for churches in a city with hundreds of them. St. Stephen's won my allegiance by dint of being so close; off we went in our snowsuits while Calvin remained a lump in the bed, recovering from a night of sin and debauchery at a viola concert at Massey Hall.

Sunday school at St. Stephen's took place after a procession, two prayers and a hymn, which children shared with the general congregation. After that, a handful of kids would rise and straggle toward the choir door, leaving behind a dozen adults scattered thinly across the pews. I found it a bit disheartening to attend this church, for it was not unlike being part of the meager audience at a poorly reviewed play. Nevertheless, having decided that this was my spiritual community, I dutifully accompanied Lester on the trip downstairs. This was our new routine, our new leaf turned, him and me going to church.

Down we went to the basement room full of toys, pots of paint and a piano, feeling righteous and simply curious, respectively. Following the lead of others, we sat down on teensy plastic chairs arranged in a circle. Three acne-scarred teenagers stood around alertly—a Christian youth trio here to assist Andrew, the teacher.

You wonder, sometimes, who becomes a Sunday-school teacher. Whether they have a facility with children, or they feel obliged, or what. Because certainly in this day and age, it isn't a totally obvious thing to volunteer for. Andrew, I noticed, seemed decidedly uncomfortable. In some ways, he was an absolutely classic Canadian WASP of the church-going variety: mild-mannered, stiff-jointed, possessing not even a wisp of charisma, attired in corduroy pants and plaid shirt, and struggling visibly with the mission of interesting small children in lessons from the Bible. But was he *innately* impaired in his teaching, I wondered, or was it the result of his ambivalence? Did his wife make him do this?

In any event, at the start of each class Andrew invited the children to light candles for his miniature altar. He handed a wooden match to the first child in the queue— for all children will instantly line up for the opportunity to play with fire—and then went rigid with fear, convinced that the church was going to go up in flames. He bent over each child with his two hands clutched like chicken claws around the match, visibly sweating, and then repeated the ritual seven times.

I like to imagine Andrew coming up with this idea of the candles and feeling almost giddy with relief at discovering something creative to do with children, before actually undertaking the task. Once the altar had been lit, Andrew generally launched into a Bible reading, upon which basis he would then have the children do some sort of craft. Here I should append a note to parents considering Sunday school: the vexing surprise is that there is no official Day One. The story never unfolds in chronological order. Your know-nothing child doesn't get to start at the beginning, with God creating the world. He dives, instead, into baffling, out-of-context lessons and discussions about mysterious characters who primarily engage in agriculture.

"Boys and girls?" Andrew would begin, experimentally testing his command of the room. "Today we're going to talk about Job and the fig tree.

"Lo, and God said to Job . . ."

Afterwards, I'd have to explain to Lester what "lo" means, and who Job was.

Perhaps the language of the Bible should be updated a touch, if only for the sake of our children. I only say this because words dating back to the reign of King James, son of Mary, Queen of Scots, do tend to complicate simple tales for children more used to reading *Walter the Farting Dog.* Consider the word "lo," which doesn't come up that often in modern conversations. I'm not even sure that I know what it means. I told Lester that it was the ancient version of "yo," but I wouldn't defend that to a theologian. With nineteenth-century classics, like Mother Goose, I can simultaneously translate as I read, turning six pence into a dollar if I need to and that sort of thing. But biblical language defies me. After a few Sunday-school sessions, I tried using biblical language around the house to see if I could just get used to it, like practicing French, or a cockney accent. In this manner, I would relay the day's events to Calvin:

"'And lo,' I said unto Lester, 'thou shalt not make a triple-decker sandwich with cream cheese and icing sugar, because thou wilt not eat it, and it will wasteth the bread.'

"And Lester said unto me, 'Yea, though I shalt not eat it truly, I shalt give it to Daddy as a present.'

"'No-est,' I saith. 'Daddy will not want it. He dost not like sandwiches made of cream cheese and icing sugar, and thus he shall cast it away as boxes of Tuna Helper upon the waters of the Nile. And there will be no bread for toast tomorrow, before daycare.'"

"Are you taking Lester tomorrow, or am I?" Calvin would reply, watching hockey on TV and not listening to me at all.

Andrew was frequently interrupted by his own son, John, an exuberant ten-year-old who obviously knew Bible stuff inside and out and had an instinct for livening things up. This made Andrew furious.

"John?" Andrew would say, his voice as taut as a mountaineer's cable, "There's only *one* teacher here today . . ."

"John? Please face the right way in your chair."

"John? If you don't settle down, you'll have to stay here while the others go into the kitchen and make the cookies."

Each remonstration was enunciated in a voice so deliberately soft, so forcibly sing-song that you just knew Andrew wanted to explode into violence. Particularly, you understood this because his son was barely obstreperous by anyone's standards, and could mostly stand accused of sensing his father's insecurity and choosing to push the big red button in his psyche marked DO NOT PUSH.

"Momma," Lester asked me after Sunday in February, "why can angels see God, but I can't see him?"

"Well," I answered, having wondered that very thing myself, "people do still see God, honey, I'm pretty sure. It's just that, ever since we left the garden and got lost in the woods, it seems like it's harder to find him."

"I bet I can find him," Lester said, taking on the challenge. "I'll leave food out for him, like we did for Santa."

"Okay, hon." I squeezed his shoulders through my mitts, game to entertain his sense of hope. My mind flew to the to-do-list challenge of remembering to eat whatever food Lester left out for God in the kitchen tonight. Who needs cocaine to make reality precarious? Try being a parent. Pile lies upon lies, artifice upon wish, Tooth Fairy upon Santa Claus upon God, all of them whisking away their proffered gifts at midnight until the time, the one time, Momma plain *forgets* and the cosmology comes crashing down.

"When you get home from the Horseshoe Tavern tonight," I reminded Calvin later that day, "don't forget to turn off the porch light and eat God's food."

15

One Sunday morning, I found myself in an unexpected conversation with a fellow named Don Yancy. I'd wandered into the after-service church social, hoping to grab something to eat while I waited for Lester, and a mutual acquaintance introduced Mr. Yancy to me as "a marvelous son-of-a-gun who had a near-death experience in Costa Rica." This description made Mr. Yancy blush furiously.

"Wow," I said, after our mutual acquaintance turned to join another conversation, "that's so amazing."

"Well, yeah, I mean, it's . . ." Mr. Yancy shrugged. "I am not afraid of death."

"No?" I marveled.

"That is so liberating, my friend," he said.

"Oh, it must be," I said, greatly envious. "I mean, in a way, it's the ultimate freedom. I can't imagine."

"No, you can't. You cannot. It's changed my life. Death has changed life. Ironic, no?"

"Yes." I smiled. "Yeah, very much so. "

He gazed off into the middle distance, contemplating how his life had been changed in the rain forest. The airy, oak-floored hall echoed with parishioners' voices as they chatted and clattered their coffee cups. Mr. Yancy was panda-shaped and clown-coiffed, his bald pate ringed with frizzed brown hair. He wore square black glasses and stood very still, his arms hanging at his sides.

"So, tell me what happened," I prompted. "You were in Costa Rica with your wife and you got bitten by a termite?"

"Nooo," said Mr. Yancy. "You're not going to have a near-death experience with a termite, my friend. That's unlikely."

"Oh, I'm sorry." I ran my hand self-consciously through my hair. "What was it?"

"It was a black widow spider. Very lethal, those critters. It bit me on the leg."

I awaited further elaboration. He shifted his gaze to me, and then away again, as if to indicate that it would be my task to animate him further, to pull a string on his lower back, or wind him up or belt him.

"So, after that happened . . ." I ventured, encouragingly.

"Yeah. And all I remember is this intense flare of red-hot pain. Like, ouch!" He mimed grabbing at his leg. "And Marci, my wife, says I dropped to the ground and started convulsing."

"Oh no," I murmured.

"I don't actually remember that. I'm sure it wasn't pretty. Like, sometimes I worry that I was lying there writhing in my shorts and maybe somebody saw . . ." His voice faltered. After a moment's hesitation, he soldiered on. "But I just—I was in pain and then I wasn't—I was floating above myself in a swirl of green. I was hovering in the rain-forest canopy, really, is what it felt like, like a hummingbird, only not like that because I wasn't darting around, I was looking down at Marci and thinking, 'Wow, she doesn't notice that I'm up here, she thinks I'm still in that body.'"

"Wow, indeed," I said. Starving, I tried to bite into a crusty sandwich yet peer respectfully at Mr. Yancy over the edges of the bread. You have to give someone your full, solemn attention when they're imparting a spiritual experience.

"Oh yeah. It was indescribable. I mean, where was I?" His arms suddenly shot up over his head as if I'd barked at him. "Where the hell was I?"

I gazed back at him, shaking my head in sympathetic wonderment.

"Well," he answered himself, "I did not know. I mean, this was my first time out of Canada. I bought a return trip from Toronto to San Jose and stopped off in the Fourth Dimension." He let out a happy, surprised guffaw. "Anyway, then I saw this light." His eyes slid back to me, seeking permission to continue.

"What kind of light?"

"I'm sure you've heard about that before, right? How people see a light that grows from a pinprick in the distance and then surrounds them."

I nodded. "Was there not—you didn't go through a tunnel?"

"What?"

"Isn't there supposed to be a tunnel?"

"No, no, there wasn't one, some people—in fact, a lot of people—go through tunnels, but I didn't." He pushed at his glasses and shrugged lightly, as if embarrassed by this small defect in his experience. "One guy I know didn't go through a tunnel either, he just had his clothes torn off by demons. Then he prayed: 'Though I walk through the valley of the shadow of death,' that prayer? And Jesus pulled him into the light.

"Anyway," he continued, now fully relaxed, "this light was so incredibly radiant, it was like . . ." he held his hands up in front of his face as if framing something, "but it didn't hurt my eyes, it wasn't a glaring light. It was just . . . it was warm, and it was enveloping and I realized that I was really a part of it, actually, which is very hard to describe, my friend. But I was at one with the universe. And that was the way it should be."

"That is so cool."

"It was. But then a voice told me it wasn't time. I don't know whose voice, but I like to think it was Jesus. That's what I believe."

At this, he lapsed back into silence and clasped his hands, his gaze returning to the middle distance. It occurred to me that Mr. Yancy was deeply shy, and that if he hadn't found God and begun coming to church, he wouldn't have said anything at all by noon on a given Sunday.

Step out into the world of belief, and you begin to see how faith is a secret that is hidden in plain view. Look for it amongst your friends and colleagues, and you glimpse it as a discernible shape within the shadows of the secular world. Before anything was asked of me—as Father McPhee had put it—I had tended to break my world into two rough camps. On the right: fundamentalists of all persuasions, using God as a force to condemn me for my blunders. On the left: agnostics, who were just a lazier version of atheists, in that they apparently had neither time nor inclination to consider God at all.

I'd never probed for shades of gray. That rarest of questions at parties. Tell me—in addition to these disclosures you're offering about your marriage, and your botched liposuction and your addiction to Dristan—do you believe in God? It just wasn't done, as they used to say.

"Do you still have the same job?" I asked Mr. Yancy. "Since this happened?"

"Well, I used to be the Webmaster for a Jeff Goldblum fan site," he replied, "and I don't do that any more. I understand that, now, to be idolatry. I mean, I don't think I was sent back to this world to continue worshipping a movie star. I feel like the scales fell from my eyes on that one. But I do still work as a Web designer. Now, I make sites for churches, mostly. Like this one. St. Stephen's."

"Oh, that's interesting," I said, but then I couldn't think of how it was interesting, really, compared to floating above the rain forest as a disembodied soul.

"I have to collect my son from downstairs," I added. "But it was very nice to talk to you, Mr. Yancy. You're a very lucky person."

He nodded and smiled. "Maybe I'll see you again."

In Sunday school, Lester had painted something passably resembling a fruit tree. A vertical stroke of brown paint. A cloud of green. Some apple-red dashes and dots.

"Adam and Eve ate apples for dinner," he explained, holding up his art work with both hands, "even though God said they weren't allowed! So then God got mad and chased them out of his garden."

"Like Mr. McGregor and Peter Rabbit," I offered, holding his hand as we ducked out of the church and turned right on Argyle Street, soft-shoeing over iced sidewalks.

16

Calvin was not as impressed as I was by Don Yancy's revelation, and did not believe, as I did, that it was worth phoning Bernice at the hospital simply to tell her that some guy I'd met in Toronto knew for sure there was a Heaven. Good news! She really *was* knocking on Heaven's Door.

"No," he said.

"No?"

"No."

We were doing the dishes, which consisted of him washing, rinsing, drying, and putting them away, and me watching.

"So you don't believe that Don Yancy's consciousness separated from his body?" I said, to be sure.

"No. I don't." He squeezed out the dishcloth.

"Why not?" I gave a little hop of indignation. "Why do

you have to pooh-pooh everything, Calvin, and be so bleak and so . . ." I bit down on my thumbnail, "so mono-syllabic?" Could my life not feature more *voluble* men?

"What other questions have you got?" Calvin asked tersely. "Because I don't have a lot of time here, I'm very busy doing all of the housework."

I sighed loudly, angry. "Okay. So you don't think there's life after death."

"I think we live, and then we die." He tossed some freshly rinsed knives into the drainer. Wiped his hands on a dishtowel. Examined a water stain on his soccer shirt.

"You don't believe that human beings have a spiritual purpose?" I cocked my head. He pulled a bottle of Beck's out of the fridge and twisted off the top. Took a swig.

"Human beings are just ants who have learned how to drive."

I threw up my hands. "You are so nihilistic, Calvin. Jesus."

I don't know why it suddenly mattered. But then I thought, there is parenting at stake. "You should be ashamed of yourself, gobbling up God's food if you think Lester should be a good little cynic." In agitation I grabbed a handful of spoons from the drainer and put them away, slamming the drawer shut. I reached for the mugs.

Calvin stood back, crossed his arms and appraised me with a smile. "You're so tidy when you're mad."

Goof. Meany. How did I wind up living with a man of such impeccable cynicism? Luck? Fate, or taste? A man who had legally changed his name from Patrick to Calvin as a direct retort to his mother's Catholicism—though he claimed it was because he didn't want to struggle through life as Pat Puddie. And what a liar. If we were just ants who had learned to drive, then why had Calvin been convinced last year that his father was trying to send him a message from the Other Side? Hmmm? Has he conveniently forgotten that episode, shortly after Stan died, when a crow flew in through our front door, and then sat on the fireplace mantel as if it were a geegaw? *Just* like the shiny ceramic crow that Stan kept on his mantelpiece in New Waterford? Like that geegaw? And Calvin murmured, "This is my father's doing."

Ants who drive, my foot.

As it happened, a few nights later, we caught a new show on Fox Television that worked nicely, I thought, as an illustration of Calvin's need to place his faith in Nothing rather than admit his yearning for the traces and echoes of a love left behind.

The show was called *Fact Factor*, and featured "the world's most extreme debates." Naturally, after that tag line, Calvin got up on his hands and knees and began crawling across the bed to grab the remote and change the channel. But I said, "Wait, Calvin, wait."

Calvin had his thumb poised over the button.

"No, no, don't. They're doing the Shroud of Turin, I want to see this."

"The Shroud . . ." said the show's announcer, totally over the top, pronouncing the word as if he were play-growling at a Vegas show girl, "what is it, really? A relic of God? Or a trick of man? Join the debate. Tonight. On *Fact Factor."*

Calvin crawled back across the bed, growling softly to himself, "The Shhhherrowddd. Yeee-ow. Here comes the Shhheerowdd."

"Shush," I advised.

The Shroud of Turin demands full attention. I feel this way because, really, *how is it possible* that a faded, ratty length of linen from France could stymie dozens of top-notch scientists for *decades,* in spite of all their spectroscopes and microscopes and MRIs? No matter how sophisticated their tests, apparently they still cannot figure out whether this thing is a work of medieval tie-dye or the cloth that enshrouded the dead body of Jesus Christ. That commands my respect. If it is just a medieval hoax, it's the best twentieth-century science-busting medieval hoax ever dreamed up by medieval people, who surely weren't even aiming to bust twentieth-century scientists. At most, they were aiming to impress fourteenth-century Christendom, and here I would be thinking of a populace that believed the world was flat, and that sin caused cancer. Not too, too hard to pull the wool over their eyes, I wouldn't think.

"Okay," Calvin said, "so . . . just to confirm. Does this mean I can't watch the game between Montreal and Boston?"

"Correct."

And then again, what if it *is* the burial cloth of Jesus Christ? What then? Well, I'm not actually sure what then.

From my own selfish point of view, the What Then is that I would finally have something objectively true to tell Lester about "what happened to that guy." He was buried! And we have his shroud!

Calvin abruptly guffawed with laughter. On the TV, two aging scholars in sweaters and Wallabees were walking manfully toward the camera in slow motion, pumped to begin their first challenge, which entailed answering the question:

Blood? Or paint?

"Tonight's scholars are bitterly opposed to one another's position on the significance of the reddish stains that cover the Shroud of Turin," explained the announcer in his weird, hubba-hubba voice. "Josh Nelson, an investigator with the Committee for the Scientific Investigation into Claims of the Paranormal, says it's paint."

"I don't just *say* it's paint," said Nelson, staring irritably into the camera. "It *is* paint."

"Why do you say that, Josh?" asked the announcer, now materializing on screen.

"Well, look," said Nelson, a guy with trim mustache and receding chin. "I have observed microanalyses that conclusively show that the 'blood' and 'body' images were rendered in tempera paint." He flashed a mirthless smile. "These die-hard Shroud enthusiasts just keep chasing the Holy Grail with pseudo-science, faulty logic and the suppression of historical facts."

"Okay, Josh," said the announcer, "but Hans Schumacher, one of Europe's leading forensic chemists, says it's blood."

Schumacher, who was small, stout and bald, defensively straightened his shoulders, smarting from the accusation that he was a pseudo-scientist. He glared across a replica of the Shroud that was laid out on a table between him and Nelson. "There is no doubt at all in my mind that what we see here are traces of blood," he said between clenched teeth.

"Why blood, Hans?"

"I will tell you why." He gestured stiffly at the cloth. "I have successfully replicated the chemical analyses done by your own American scientists, Dr. Heller and Dr. Adler, and once again, I have firmly established the presence of the bile pigment bilirubin, a porphyrin fluorescence, and the substances hemochromogen and cyanmethemoglobin. These are all blood properties that you simply do not see with paint."

Calvin and I were staring at the TV now in a lax, uncomprehending stupor.

The two men plunged into a heated exchange about whether one would or would not expect to see the release of nitrogen gas bubbles in a particular kind of test done on ancient blood. Nelson cited earlier tests by famed "microanalyst" McCrone, who had not found the telltale nitrogen bubbles. He crossed his arms languidly and leaned back in his chair. "McCrone wrote the whole thing off twenty years ago as a medieval forgery, and here we are still having to talk about it."

"McCrone," retorted Schumacher, visibly reddening, "failed to perform controls with artificially aged blood. He failed to check the possibility that nitrogen gas will not be produced by very aged, strongly denatured blood samples."

"Okay, smartass," Nelson shot back, "why is the blood red? If it's two thousand years old, it should be dark brown."

"The blood is not whole blood, you fool! " burst out Schumacher. "It is exudate from a blood clot. You must work with what you know of the circumstances. If you beat a man, and scourge him, and then nail him up to a cross, you will destroy red blood cells! And the cell debris will go to the liver! And be converted there into the bile pigment bilirubin!"

"You see, Calvin? That's my point," I said, settling smugly back against my pillows.

"No, I don't see. What is your point?"

"My point is that a medieval hoaxer would have been as likely to paint the Shroud to look like phlegm, choler or bile, right? Because those were the four humors that they thought flowed through the body. So what are the odds that he or she used paint to mimic the pigment bilirubin?"

"Gosh, I don't know." He got out of bed and padded down the hallway. I heard the click of the bathroom-door lock. After the commercial, Josh Nelson began arguing that the real Shroud of Christ would have been made of several pieces of linen, not just one.

"The Shroud contradicts the Gospel of John," he barked, "which describes multiple cloths, as well as 'an hundred pound weight' of burial spices—not a trace of which appears on this thing."

119

"Ach, that's rich, coming from a professional skeptic," retorted Schumacher. "You wouldn't recognize Moses if he parted your soup, and now you argue that the Shroud is inauthentic because of the Gospel of John. A skeptic turning to the Bible for proof!" Schumacher shook his head and threw up his chubby arms, turning angrily to the host. "Now I have seen everything."

Oh, I said to myself, since Calvin was still in the bathroom, touché. That's a very good point. There's a skeptic so obsessed with upholding his skepticism that he turns to the Bible. As orthodox in his skepticism as a born-again Christian.

"Can we watch the hockey game now?" Calvin asked, rematerializing in the doorway and swan-diving onto the bed. "If you're into blood sport, I guarantee you hockey's more interesting."

What Calvin despised, it seemed to me, as I puzzled it out in the darkness that night while he snored, is how people make such fools of themselves in their quest for meaning. He was afraid of that. His best defense against heartbreak and sorrow was to dismiss hope. Illusions could only be shattered.

17

At work on Monday morning, I tried Don Yancy's conversion in Costa Rica out on Avery, hoping for a more enthusiastic response.

"Ho," he exclaimed, twisting his arms and scratching his neck, "hmmm. At least he didn't claim that angels danced on his teeth."

I stared at him.

"That's not a very compelling counterargument, Avery."

"No, I suppose it isn't."

We both started laughing.

"I haven't read any literature on NDEs," Avery reflected, "but I imagine the argument could be made, uhh, that they fall within the Gnostic tradition. An experiential knowledge of God that you can neither prove nor disprove."

"Why not? Why can't you disprove it?" I leaned forward on my elbows and tapped my pencil against my chin.

"Well . . ." Avery toyed with an elastic band as he thought of how to put it. "If I said that I loved you, and you said, 'Prove it,' how would I? How would I prove it?"

I mulled this over for the rest of the morning, as I thumbed through new books and jotted down notes about whom I might call to review them. How could someone prove love?

That afternoon, the hallway in our building was abuzz with the news that the *Moral Volcano* had lost its bushy-bearded senior editor, Leonard Greenberg. It was a major blow. Greenberg was a star. A former opera critic whose innate snobbishness had drawn him to the *Volcano* at its much hoo-hawed inception, he had flourished in the ensuing months as an editor and columnist, displaying the talent of an idiot savant in his singular ability to ridicule liberals. But now, at least according to the gossip, Greenberg had done an abrupt volte-face and was running off to start a blog excoriating his former conservative friends, apparently after being trapped in the elevator at Robarts Library for several hours during a power outage with a kind, knock-kneed opera-buff librarian liberal, who soothed Greenberg's claustrophobic panic by humming arias from Humperdinck's *Hänsel und Gretel*.

By late afternoon, the *Volcano*'s editor-in-chief, Sherman O'Sullivan, having looked around wildly for a replacement editor, suddenly discovered me. I heard later that he learned through the grapevine that I had edited at New York's *Pithy Review* some years earlier before coming home to raise Lester. For Torontonians, word of a gig in New York invariably trumps all other considerations, such as competence, and thus O'Sullivan immediately trotted down the hall and knocked on our door.

Avery, tipped back in his wooden swivel chair, glanced up from his reading when he heard a loudly cleared throat, and then gazed at me with a sly and expectant smile. Lo, it is Sherman O'Sullivan, declared Avery's expression: he of the impeccable suits and boyish face whose blue eyes are so round and ingenuous that they must have been stolen from the Gerber baby. That happy child-man we have often discussed.

"I'm sorry to intrude," O'Sullivan said, smiling brightly. Beads of perspiration dotted his forehead, from which his blond hair was swept back in an insouciant wave.

"Oh, hello," I said in surprise. "Have you run out of coffee? We have tons, if you need some."

"I have sufficient coffee, thank you," said O'Sullivan. "What I lack just at the moment is an editor."

Avery and I stared back, uncertain what he meant by reporting this to us.

"What I mean to say," Sherman added, offering me another warm smile—he tended to trust in his own boyish charm—"is that I would be very obliged if I could discuss the possibility of some . . ." He shifted his gaze to the floor and shook his head, as if he couldn't quite believe the absurdity of his predicament. "Well. Emergency editing, I guess."

"You need an extra pair of hands down the hall?" I asked.

"Yes, I do, I do need that," he glanced about our office. "Of course I will arrange for suitable compensation. I don't expect you to perform a favor." He gestured vaguely back toward his own office. "I need a pair of experienced eyes. A read-through of my editor's letter. Hilary would do it, but she's up to her eyeballs, and Leonard was the one I always trusted with the task."

I crossed my arms. "You want me to do this because I used to edit Paul Graham's work in New York, is that why?"

O'Sullivan brought his hands together, tilted his head and smiled. "Suffice it to say that I would very much like to borrow you, Frances, for a bit of untended editorial business."

I shot a questioning look at Avery, who bent his head and busied himself winding his watch.

"Alright," I offered, tentative. It flew through my mind that the *Moral Volcano* might net me some extra cash, and that could not hurt me. Our own publisher, Iris McKeen, had turned eighty this year and paid little attention to the *Dandelion Review* beyond funding it in honor of her bookish deceased husband, Ed.

That night I stayed up late, sitting cross-legged on the fold-out futon couch in my living room, laboring over O'Sullivan's column. He was pooh-poohing liberals, as was his wont.

"Apparently," he had written, and I inserted punctuation as I read, "the liberal approach to foreign affairs leaves experienced warriors at the Pentagon cold. Shivering, one might even say. For this, if I may summarize, is liberals' foreign policy: in military defeat, appeal to Europe. In military victory, run for a hug from the Russians. To capture terrorists, go crying to the French. When dictators are caged, turn them over to Europe's princes of power for a slap on the wrist." Whereupon he concluded: "Deep down, liberals are just Euro-weeny traitors. They yearn to surrender everything to the French."

Rubbing my forehead, I thought about how to edit this for what we, in the business, call sense. Editing for sense. You put small queries in the margin, such as "Is this the right sense of 'appeal'?" Although I wasn't a foreign-policy analyst, I had not observed any American liberals attempting to appeal to the governments of Europe concerning American defense policy. Better to use a word like "noticed"? They "noticed" the Europeans? Or "consulted"? Or "thought to confer with" them? I provided these alternatives in the margin. Then I suddenly wondered, did he mean that liberals were appealing, *were attractive*, to Europeans?

Also, I worried over his last sentence: "They yearn to surrender everything to the French." Could this be construed as accurate? The French once turned over Louisiana. Was this a turning-back over to them of Louisiana, and other territory, strictly speaking, or was "everything" a metaphor for turning over the reins of

125

sovereign decision-making? In either case, it was a striking allegation. Getting up from the futon and shaking out
my leg, which had fallen asleep, I decided that
O'Sullivan was probably just speaking metaphorically.
To err on the side of caution, though, I circled the word
"everything" and wrote in the margin: "More specific?"

I went to bed, let my mind wander, and began wondering how Don Yancy would be greeted by a neo-
conservative. Would the fellows down the hall applaud
him for having found God? Were they *religious?* I had
assumed that their tendency to describe daycare as
"socialist warehousing" arose from some sort of cosmology. But in truth, I had never asked.

18

At last, a phone call from Bernice's oncologist.

Calvin answered in the kitchen, and I listened on the extension in our bedroom, lying down, legs scissored half in and half out of my duvet, watching CNN with the sound off. Lester made roaring noises in the hall, where he'd set up his African animals with a roasting pan full of water for the hippos. The news scrolled by on the bottom of the TV screen, out of synch with Wolf Blitzer's dour expression, since he was apparently divulging news about Iraq, whereas the bottom of the screen was revealing that Paris Hilton had lost her chihuahua.

"Alright," said Dr. Pereira, in a voice that sounded hoarse with fatigue, "sorry for the delay, but I am one of only two oncologists on the island of Cape Breton, which has, as you may know, the highest cancer incidence in

Canada. If you wish, you might complain to your MP. I have certainly done so, myself." He paused, perhaps scanning the chart in front of him. "So. Ah yes. Your mother. I see. She did very well in the surgery."

"The surgery," Calvin repeated dryly.

"Yes, of course, the surgery."

"And what surgery would that be?" I could picture Calvin slouching over the table in the kitchen below me, trying to swallow his raging frustration.

"Oh," said Dr. Pereira, sounding surprised. "I see. Your mother did not discuss this surgery with you?"

"Uh, no. She didn't mention it the other day."

"I see. Well, she is recovering very well. We removed her right arm from immediately below the humerus, and, I believe, successfully excised the malignancy from its primary site in the bone."

"You cut my mother's *arm off?*"

"Yes. Oh. No." Dr. Pereira clucked his tongue. "I see. Your mother is not Bernice Potter?"

"No."

"Oh. Yes. No. One moment. Forgive me. I have not been reviewing the correct chart." There was a rustling of paper. "If I may clarify, your mother still has two arms?"

"Yes! She does! As a matter of fact, I was really hoping that I could finally have a conversation about my mother and what's wrong with her that didn't revolve around her fucking arms. You have no idea how sick to death I am of my mother and her arms. So, please, find the chart for Bernice *Puddie*, and tell me something that does not include the word 'arm'."

128

"But we can certainly talk about her legs," I interjected, worried that Calvin's outburst would put the oncologist off of limbs generally, and there Bernice was all swollen up and hobbled.

"I see," Dr. Pereira said after a paper-rustling pause. "Have I removed your mother's legs, then?"

"Oh for Chrissake," said Calvin, "can you just consult your notes?"

"Yes, yes, of course. I can review the correct chart and call you back. That's no trouble."

"NO!" shouted Calvin. "No, please don't hang up. If you hang up, you'll get busy and you won't phone me back for weeks, and I've got a job, and I need to figure out my schedule, and my aunt is being useless, and I can't—I need to know what is wrong with my mother. Now. That doesn't involve her arms."

Dr. Pereira complied. For a while, all we heard was the contemplative in-and-out click of his ballpoint pen. At last, he exhaled loudly and began.

"So. Yes. Your mother's primary cancer has metastasized from the breast, and the CT scans tell me that it has now seeded throughout her abdomen. Into a number of organs. This is a difficult predicament. We treated her with tamoxifen, and that eventually ran its course of efficacy, and then I assigned her Femara, which also ceased to work after a time, so I am now recommending fulvestrant, which sells under the brand-name Faslodex. This is a treatment for hormone-receptor-positive metastatic breast cancer in post-menopausal women whose disease has progressed, following anti-estrogen therapy. You should know it has certain side effects, the most common of which are pharyngitis, peripheral edema, vasodilatation and asthenia. But there are a variety of drugs I can prescribe that will counter these effects, also."

"What do you mean?" Calvin asked.

"I'm sorry?"

"I'm literally trying to get the gist of this. You're saying that my mother is riddled with cancer, and you're proposing to riddle her with drugs?"

"Yes, well, Faslodex has only recently been approved, so it is difficult to predict its long-term efficacy, but your mother has responded well, for periods of time, to hormonal therapies, so it is certainly the best course of treatment in her case."

"She hides her Gaviscon in her shoes," I interjected, hoping to sound informed. "Is that okay? Or should we be pushing her to take that, as well?"

"Gaviscon is for her comfort, only. If she does not wish to take it . . ."

"And I just have another quick question," I added. "Bernice thinks she has asthma and it's swelling up her legs. That's not right, right?"

"I see. Well, a bilateral edema could be caused by systemic vasculitis, renal or liver failure, protein-losing enteropathy, or, as I mentioned, it could be a side effect of drug treatment."

"Look, Dr. Pereira, I need to get to the bottom line, here. Are my mother's chickens coming home to roost?"

"I'm sorry?"

"Is my mother dying, or is she not dying?"

"In the long run, yes, I think that you will find that Falodex is not a cure, although it is possible. But mainly I am hoping that it will give her some time."

"Time for what?"

"For what?" Dr. Pereira reiterated, sounding puzzled.

"For what?"

"For what." The doctor seemed to consider this question for a spell, and then he took a deep breath and answered, his voice soft and almost rueful, "I believe that is a question you will have to put to your mother."

19

"Endless invention, endless experiment, brings knowledge of motion, but not of stillness. . . . Where is the Life we have lost in living? Where is the wisdom we have lost in knowledge?"

It was Monday morning, and Avery was indulging in his typical routine of quoting authors out of thin air in response to my account of the weekend.

"So, who are you copping from this morning?" I asked, attempting to roll up the rim on my Tim Hortons coffee cup to see if I'd won a prize.

"T. S. Eliot," he said, ordering the papers on his desk. "'The Rock.'"

"Oh, interesting," I mused, "I was thinking about Eliot when I was out in Cape Breton at Christmas. How he made more sense to me when I was a teenager than the Church did."

"Well, Eliot was a great devotee of the Church of England," Avery offered, "but in his later years. At some point, he came around from, I suppose, agnosticism, I'm not entirely sure."

"The bastard died of emphysema, did you know that? It is perfect." So announced Goran, who was fixing himself an espresso, his wavy gray hair falling into his eyes as he bent over the little machine beside his design table. It was one of his rare days in the office.

"What do you mean, 'perfect'?" I asked. You never knew with Goran. He was fluent in English, technically, but his use of idioms was somewhat unpredictable. I'd heard him employ the word "perfect" as a catch-all for a variety of meanings, ranging from "amazing" to "ironic" to "feeling well."

How are you today, Goran? "Perfect."

How was the Pixies concert? "It was perfect."

Would ya look at that, it's snowing in August. "Yes, it is perfect."

"I mean," he said, fixing me with deep-set gray eyes that drooped along with his jowls so that he had a slight basset-hound look, "that Eliot knocked five, maybe ten years off his life by smoking. But he is memorial! The whole world knows of this man! What if he had quit smoking, like good boy, at my age?"

I wasn't sure how old Goran was. I thought perhaps forty-five, although he carried on with women and dressed like a man in his twenties.

"I ask you," Goran continued, "would he have written *Murder in Cathedral*? 'Ash-Wednesday'? Or bounced off walls for wanting to smoke, and offered nothing of genius to world?"

Goran was an adamant chain-smoker of Camels. Come to think of it, I had yet to meet an Eastern European intellectual in Toronto who gave a rat's ass about healthy living. "This mother-in-law you have," he argued, "why should she take these drugs? You say she is religious. Why not let her go to her God? She has lost her husband, you said? So, it's perfect. Don't listen to technocrats. Life should be full, and short. Write your poems, love your lovers, drink your fill. And smoke."

"Do you believe in God, Goran?" I asked, cupping my chin in my hand.

"I believe that people have right to believe in their God. My God, I have not met yet. He looks after my parents, and He waits my arrival. I look forward to our introduction." On that note, he strode off to suck on a Camel in the stairwell.

"What about you, Avery?" I asked, feeling bold, for we usually leapt away from intimate questions and communicated, instead, through anecdote and quote.

"Well, uhh," he replied, his arms beginning to make their serpentine moves, "it's a complicated subject for Monday morning, Frannie."

"Oh, sure, and that's coming from you, who throws poetry at me before I've finished my coffee," I retorted. "Can't you just say yes or no?"

Avery tilted back in his chair and wouldn't look at me. He was discomfited. He didn't want to discuss this, which made me regret that I'd pressed.

"Maybe there's a God," he allowed, "but if there is, then He or She took away my mother, and didn't leave a note. I'm not looking as forward as Goran is, I suppose I could say, to being introduced to this Mighty Being."

"Right," I said, dropping my eyes to my desk.

At lunch, alone in the diner and bored by the paper, I began thinking about T. S. Eliot again. How he'd once filled the void I felt between the inanities of my secular culture—where we all swung our teen heads, drunk on vodka, to Joan Jett belting out "I love rock and roll"—and the Church's bland counterpoint. I was adrift until I came ashore at the elegant *cri de coeur* that was Eliot's *The Waste Land*. A call to arms. Or a great huge sigh. Not that I had a nitwit's grasp of what he was saying. I came across Eliot in grade twelve English, at the same time, by coincidence, that the sweaty mound of Marlon Brando in *Apocalypse Now* quoted from "The Hollow Men," which instantly reinforced my attraction to Eliot by indirect association with my crush on Martin Sheen.

"We are the tin men, we are the hollow men, foreheads stuffed with straw. Ha ha." I can't remember exactly how it goes.

Eliot appealed enormously to my overblown sense of alienation at the time. I quoted him sagaciously to my friends whenever we complained of the weather: "April is the cruelest month, breeding lilacs out of the dead land." Nods all around. That was, like, so true! You kept thinking, okay here comes spring, and then not!

Of course, Eliot was all about the ambiguous conflation of offended intellect and bad mood, and that wasn't, technically, the same thing as religion. But there was his evocation of despair—sterile thunder, dry bones rattling, the polluted Thames, the jarring emptiness of a one-night stand. I made great, teenaged hay out of those images, flinging them about as melodramatic retorts to lousy dates and high school cliques. And somewhere within it all, I had a glimpse, however confused and hesitant, of the divine: *"Who is that other walking beside you?"*

The idea that there was more than earthbound life—a sparkling heaven, a sense of grace—was something that I understood, but could make no sense of. Heaven seemed far too convenient. It was my Protestant roots that entangled me with skepticism, I felt. Protestantism confounded itself by being too suspicious of reward. Cake, maybe, if you bake it yourself and don't waste a crumb. Otherwise, dry bones rattling.

It would be years and years—in fact, until I was confronted by Lester—until I began to get a certain idea that had eluded me before: that you had to work, spiritually, to reach a state of grace. It wasn't like Santa Claus handing me the gift of eternity. It wasn't *about* me at all.

20

Here is a hard-earned mother's tip. I shall whisper it, for fear of hurting Calvin's feelings.

If your child is experiencing a transition, such as attending a new school, moving into a new house, or witnessing an illness in the family, do not shave your head.

This was Lester's reaction to Calvin's whimsical styling choice:

"Daddy, *where's your hair?*" he burst out in shocked horror when I brought him home from daycare and he spied his father in the kitchen, reading *Rolling Stone.* Calvin's thick nut-brown locks had been shorn at the barber by impulsive request.

"You're *disgusting!*" Lester wailed, thoroughly undone. He fled the kitchen and shut himself in the bathroom, still in full winter apparel, sobbing. "Go away!" he shrieked, when I tried to follow him.

Perhaps a less extreme haircut had been in order.

"What did you do that for?" I demanded of Calvin, returning to the kitchen in a fury. I'd caught Lester's reaction like a flu bug.

"What?" he protested in dismay, patting his bald pate. "I hate having hat hair in the winter, it drives me nuts. So I shaved my head for the time being, so what?"

"So what?" I echoed, incredulous. "It looks totally alarming!"

"What on earth did you do to your head?" asked my mother, who walked in a few moments behind me carrying a bag of books.

"I see I'm a big hit," Calvin muttered, getting up to retrieve his Toronto Blue Jays cap from the hook behind the door.

My mother, bundled up in her camel-hair coat and a fur-trimmed hat that looked like a winterized trilby, brushed snowflakes from her shoulders and placed her bag on the table. "Here are some more library books for Lester. Frannie, have you read him Roald Dahl yet? I was hoping not."

"No, not yet. Thanks," I said, distracted. "Calvin, go talk to him. Don't just leave him crying in there."

My mother looked up alertly, suddenly conscious of the sounds of her grandson. "Have you and Lester had words?"

"Well, I wouldn't put it that way," Calvin said, adjusting his cap in the mirror above the sink. "He came home and found a bald man where his father used to be."

"Ah," said my mother, loosely clasping her gloved hands. "Well, it's not at all surprising that you upset him.

Young children can be very frightened by that kind of physical transformation. They don't yet have a clear distinction between reality and fantasy—between what is possible and impossible. To him, you might be in the process of changing completely and, the next thing, your arms will disappear or what have you."

"Oh, *please* don't talk to me about arms," Calvin said, sitting down heavily at the table and holding his head between his hands.

"Do you remember, Frannie," my mother asked, "when your father and I were watching that Japanese film, *Spirits Gone Away*, and you came in with Lester and he was so terribly upset by the little girl's parents being transformed into pigs?"

"It was called *Spirited Away*, Mum," I said, still listening to Lester's muffled sobs, which seemed to be calming down a bit.

"Well, that's the sort of image that really scares a child," she continued. "We expect them to be afraid of dinosaurs and monsters, but that's not it at all. Calvin, you need to go and show him that you're still the same. Let him feel your head."

"Okay, okay," said Calvin, heading for the bathroom with an air of resignation. My mother gave me a wintry kiss, her cheeks still ice-cold from her walk, and reminded me to come for dinner on the weekend. When the door had closed behind her, I took off my coat and pulled a Kraft Super Deluxe pizza out of the freezer.

"Aw, come on, Les," I heard Calvin cajole in the bathroom, "don't be so sad. I just wanted to look more like

Caillou. He's bald, isn't he? And nothing else about him changes, does it? He runs around in his little cartoon world being earnest and having adventures, and the plot never develops—"

"What about Grandpa?" Lester interrupted. "He changed."

"What do you mean, little man?" I could hear a flicker of discomfort in Calvin's voice.

"He changed, Daddy! *All* of him changed. Granny says he turned into an angel. And now nobody can see him any more."

"Oh, well . . ." Calvin replied lightly, hoping to dismiss this case in point. "That's different."

"Why?"

"Because it's *different,* Les." The upset in his voice was obvious. "I'm not going to die tomorrow just because I shaved off my hair today. I'm not leaving you, I won't suddenly disappear like that and leave you alone with your mum."

"How do you know?"

"I just know, okay?"

The air changed. I could feel it, and so could Lester, the way children uncannily sense when it's time for them to compose themselves and let the grown-up be the sad one. "I didn't say Grandpa disappeared," Lester offered, wanting to correct the record so that Calvin would feel reassured. "He didn't disappear, Daddy. His soul is in my heart."

I drew in my breath sharply and leaned back against the fridge. Wondrous child! Where the hell did he get that?

21

Here is a list of activities you can enjoy with your five-year-old in Canada during the winter, when a freak thunderstorm that some blame on global warming has neatly erased all the snow.

Watch TV

Watch TV

Watch TV

Make muffins

Have a bubble bath

Color for ten minutes

Watch TV

BELIEVE ME

Walk to the neighborhood Starbucks whining constantly about how cold it is, order hot chocolate, suck the whipped-cream topping through a straw

Watch TV

22

Calvin flew back to Cape Breton for a few days to sort things out for Bernice, and Lester responded by growing despondent about the extinction of dinosaurs. Perhaps it was just a coincidence. But we were hanging out in the house, watching TV, and a documentary called *Walking with Dinosaurs* came on the Discovery Channel.

In one episode, a computer-generated asteroid came streaking down to Earth just as a young pair of T. rexes were finding their way through the cycad forests of Montana, at which point all hell broke loose.

The tyrannosaur hatchlings were blown sideways by the force of this wild impact-generated wind, and Lester watched, transfixed, from when the trail of stardust fell ominously through the twilit sky, to when Kenneth Branagh, lately employed as a narrator who horrifies children, explained the extinction of dinosaurs.

BELIEVE ME

Dinosaurs ended?

He ran to his room in hysterics. Dinosaurs cannot just have *ended;* I understood that, as a mother. They were the mainstay of my son's daily imaginative existence. This was a child who made me sit on the bed and provide nature show voice-overs involving clashes between stegosaurs and raptors as he acted out the primal conflict amidst the hills and valleys of the floral-patterned rayon comforter. For Branagh merely to pronounce them *fini,* all done, buh-bye, was incomprehensible. What did he mean to suggest? Had all the dinosaurs become angels as well?

My brain began to hurt. Couldn't I have had a normal son preoccupied with Hot Wheels? I tried to get around the crisis by pointing out that certain dinosaurs didn't end, technically, so much as evolve into birds.

"Hey, Les!" I exclaimed one morning before daycare. "Look what I've found in the news! According to new fossil finds in northeastern China, some dinosaurs grew feathers! They changed into *birds.*"

Lester raised his eyes to me, wary. I couldn't be sure if he was feeling suspicious of my tone, or the news. "It's true, beauty," I insisted, scanning the article, "paleontologists just found one of them lying splat in some rock sediment surrounded by down, fluff and feathers. Do you see what I'm saying? They didn't go extinct, this article says, they just changed into birds."

I leaned over and ruffled his dark hair. "And this is interesting: the group of dinosaurs that sprouted feathers is the theropod. Like what, Lester, what's one of the meat-eating dinosaurs?"

"Velociraptor," he offered alertly, "T. rex."

"So, there you go," I told him happily. "They didn't go extinct, they just changed."

Calvin laughed, when I explained what I'd learned when we spoke on the phone that night, caught in small daily triumphs of insight. "You're joking," he said. "Are they saying that T. rex evolved into a budgie? That's like me evolving into a spoon."

Mmm. But I suppose that's the thing about evolution. The process involves a time scale that humans cannot get their heads around. It's really more about our inability to conceive of these transformations than about what is plausible. For, given enough time, lots and lots and lots and lots of time, curmudgeons like Calvin could, theoretically, eventually evolve into something resembling a teaspoon.

Or maybe that wasn't the thing about evolution. Lester and I leafed through a piece in the *National Geographic* about flying pterosaurs who were as big as F-18 fighter jets—can you imagine?—soaring through the prehistoric mists for 125 million years. Generation after generation after generation, catching fish and mating and catching fish and mating and accumulating a knowledge base of nothing at all. And the only conceivable point of this that I can conceive of is that, eventually, a spark of intelligence caught fire somewhere on the planet and moved things along. For, after intelligence evolved, so then did sociability, and love, and playfulness and artistry and consciousness and reverence.

We won't die so much as change. Everything connects. Life goes on. Theropods become pigeons and adapt to a brave new world of bread crumbs and parkettes, and humans lead the charge—along with elephants and dolphins and chimps—of further evolution toward a consciousness of God.

"Lo," I proclaimed to Calvin, after he got home from his frustrating visit to New Waterford, where his mother refused to entertain Dr. Pereira's prognosis. "We have a physical body and a spiritual body, so saith the Bible. And just because one evolveth into the other, which is invisible—that maketh it no less plausible than prehistoric fish evolving into airplane-size reptiles that fly. What sayeth you?"

"Cut it out," said Calvin, swinging open the door of the fridge. "Did you drink all my beer while I was gone?"

"Verily. Indeed it is so."

23

In the illustrious tradition of spiritual autobiography, be it memoir by C. S. Lewis or the rapturous testimony of Julian of Norwich, the seeker invariably has a mentor, to whom he or she addresses questions of faith as the revelations unfold. "Father, what is meant by unceasing prayer?" Or "Reverend Mother, how can I banish sin when I am such a wretch?"

I needed someone to whom I could pass along questions from Lester, such as, "When I'm an angel, will I still have my eyeballs?" But I had my own yearning for answers now, too, and I felt it wouldn't be such a bad thing to have a mentor. But Andrew at Sunday school just wasn't cutting it for me. I couldn't respect a spiritual guide who clearly needed to go on Paxil. Though he was a wonderful ambulatory book of quotations, Avery was too skeptical. My best friend, Marina, who lived in New

York, told me that she did believe in God, but she also felt certain that we were merely God's Sea Monkeys, and that he'd lost interest in us and forgotten where he'd put our packet of food. "How else do you explain that angels were popping up everywhere two thousand years ago, talking to shepherds and Mary and Abraham, and yet nobody's heard from them since?" she wanted to know. A mentor wasn't supposed to be asking me the questions.

My mother was irredeemably secular, my father typically vague, and no one else of their age and wisdom seemed suitable. How had I stumbled so easily upon Father McPhee in New Waterford, I marveled now.

For the time being, the only person I could really talk to about spiritual matters in Toronto was my cousin Kate, whom I joined for Ashtanga yoga every Thursday at noon.

Kate was a lawyer. A fiercely feminist lawyer who brought off brilliant resolutions for women in divorce cases, whom Kate deemed poorly treated by oafs and control freaks. She was also a devoted Quaker, which appealed to her practical activist side, although it had taken her years of questing about to settle on a suitable framework for her beliefs. In one memorable instance, dating back to the mid-1990s, Kate embroiled me in a weekend workshop with a shaman from suburban Toronto named Larry. At the time that she instigated this scheme, we were in her New York apartment on Washington Square, while I studied at Columbia and she took her master's in law at NYU. She was reading my

Tarot cards, and puzzling out what it meant that I had received the Phoenician, upside down.

"Look, Kate," I pointed out, "you can figure out what the card means, but then you do have to concede that what you are doing is probably just imaginary."

She refused to concede any such thing, and an argument ensued in which Kate accused me of being "spiritually frigid," and this led, in turn, to my lying flat on my back, blindfolded, in a rec room in Mississauga the following summer.

"Start at the beginning," Kate had said, explaining to me why we had to go visit Larry. "With the first practices, the first principles. Begin with the universal beginning of religious quest, the shaman's journey."

"The what?" I asked.

"Shamanism, Frannie," she repeated, drawing out the syllables. "You know, Wade Davis? Carlos Castaneda? Tribal spirit work?"

"Give me another clue," I suggested.

"Shamanism is a spiritual practice which for thousands of years has been central to tribal communities. The word 'shaman' actually comes from Siberia," she added, pedantically, "but the role of an elder who can bring his people into contact with the spirit world is common from the Amazon to China."

"Oh, that's good," I said. "So who's your shaman? That psychic you told me about who wrote *Hello from Heaven*?"

"No, actually, in a way it would be the anthropologist Michael Harner. He studied in Peru, where shamans are

able to guide people into trance states by using hallucinogens and a specific drumbeat. There's something
about the brainwave frequency that the drumming tunes
people into. It allows them to perceive a different reality.
He's measured it in a lab. And it turns out that it's the
same frequency in totally different parts of the world,
like in the Amazon and in certain African tribes and the
Inuit. Harner calls shamanism the basic precedent of all
religions."

"So, if I drop acid and then listen to a drum solo I'll
come face to face with God? I could have told you that."

"No," she said, raising her brow at me, "it has to be
guided. Journeying isn't child's play."

24

Larry lived in a split-level on Sunny Day Crescent, and when we arrived a bit early for our day-long workshop that summer, we found him outside mowing his lawn.

"Hi, Larry!" Kate sing-songed out the window of her Honda.

He paused, squinting in the sunlight, and then gave her a lopsided grin. Larry was one of those men with very slim legs and tiny bums squeezed into jeans, whose look I tend to associate with Led Zeppelin concerts. Maybe it was also the mullet. He ambled toward us, wiping his hands on his shirt.

"Hey, man," Larry said, "good to see you, Kate."

We all shook hands and Larry politely refrained from completing his mowing, leaving the lawn shorn in zigzag strips, and led us through his garage, into a kitchen festooned with bongs. Nowadays, Larry noted, as he studiously measured out two spoonfuls of coffee, shamans such as himself were obliged to skip hallucinogens. But otherwise, the method remained the same. The shaman—who used to be all naked and painted, but Larry preferred to wear an oversized monk's robe— calls in the spirits through whistles, rattles and drumming, with participants arranged in a sacred circle to reinforce the energy field. Then each person "journeys" in "non-ordinary reality" until the shaman calls them back.

Kate and I sipped coffee from big white mugs at Larry's kitchen table while he went upstairs to grab his monk's robe and the other workshop participants trickled in. In strolled a couple of friends from Larry's day job at Sam the Record Man, followed by a spry woman of seventy or so who wore yoga attire, then a ponytailed fellow who looked about fifty and brought his own coffee cup, which dangled from his neck on a string. Finally, Larry's girlfriend, Tina, who was just about as thin as he was and wore similarly skintight jeans. After Larry reappeared, rubbing his hands together and saying "Hey, man" and "Thanks for coming," we all filed downstairs into the wood-paneled, shag-rugged rec room and milled about uncertainly until we sorted ourselves out in a cross-legged circle.

Larry assumed command of the room. Gazing into the center of the circle as if drawing strength from his rug, he solemnly instructed us to journey into the spirit world and attempt to locate our Power Animal. If we wished, we could ask the Animal a question. Native Americans, he explained, used to ask the spirits very specific questions, such as how to locate the bison herd, or where did So-and-So go in the canoe. I looked over at Kate, wondering if she also found that intriguing, that our ancestors just sought information—not the Meaning of Life, which they understood perfectly, but answers to the irksome daily questions that we solve by flipping on the Weather Channel or ringing people up on the phone. Kate had her eyes closed, however. I guessed she was preparing for the trip.

Larry knee-swished in his monk's robe over to his drum, and gestured to his girlfriend to pick up her rattle so that they could play the special beat that would enable us to journey into the spirit world. I began to feel nervous. I figured I would ask whatever happened to my granny. She had died in her sleep after a fine long life, but then what? On the other hand, perhaps "then what?" was too broad a query for shamanic journeying? But I couldn't think of anything else I wanted to know. As I lay down and waited, I got to wondering if the Power Animals in Non-Ordinary Reality were better at finding canoes or at providing rudiments of meaning to our lives. Maybe they felt relieved that nobody was bugging them any more about where they put their skinning knives or whether it would rain.

The drum began to beat: loud, insistent and almost dizzying—the sonic equivalent of a disco strobe. Larry said we had to imagine diving into a tree stump or a pond or something that would lead to "the lower world." After a stretch of time banging my head into solid earth,

I finally succeeded in worming down through a cave, and then suddenly found myself in a meadow. The first power animal—or figment of my imagination—to come along was a wolf. He was snarling and yellow-eyed, crouched at the edge of the meadow. I began to chase after him, and he loped into dense undergrowth. Hacking and swatting my way through the bushes in frenzied pursuit, I ran across a chipmunk, which gave me pause. Oh, hello, Thing I Have Imagined in Larry's Basement. Should I ask *you* about life after death?

I said to the chipmunk, "Where is my granny?" and it led me a merry chase, up and down trees, skittering along branches, faster and faster until my pulse raced. Then the chipmunk revealed a triptych of images: boiling, swirling clouds with Granny's distorted face in them; a cottage in a poplar grove that evoked a Russian fairy tale; her gravesite in the sweet green light of summer. Which meant what?

Larry called us back by slowing his drum beat. Sitting up, we stretched our legs, rolled our necks, reclaimed notebooks, glasses, a ballcap.

"So, okay," Larry said. "This would be the time where shamans returned from their journey, and grabbed their charcoal stick or a cup of ochre or whatever they had available, and painted what they'd seen on a sacred rock site. Right? That's the spirit of this, but my house is a rental so I can't really have people marking up the walls down here. I hope that's understandable. So we're just going to go around the circle and see what you all have to report."

Kate reported riding on the back of a great stag, swifter than the wind, which leapt high above a village full of blind men. Marcia, the elderly woman in yoga pants, declared that her power animal was a panther, with eyes like gleaming emeralds, who led her through the jungle to the sea, where a sailing ship awaited her. Larry's friend Bob explained that he'd met—and then run away from—a tarantula. "Oh, man, it was so intense," he said, close to tears. "I'm *terrified* of spiders, man." The middle-aged man with the ponytail described a magnificent killer whale who assured him that he would find love again, but only if he moved to Vancouver. Larry's other friend Chris conceded that he hadn't been able to get into the lower world at all. He had spent the entire half-hour trying to squeeze through a drain pipe.

"What about you, Fran?" asked Larry, as all eyes turned to me.

"I met a wolf," I began, wishing I could embark upon a wonderful tale, which I couldn't. "But then, actually, it went away and I wound up talking to a chipmunk. So . . . that was fine."

"Okay," said Larry, "so, let's take a break, and when we come back we'll be working with our rocks."

Later, Kate and I argued over plates of pad thai at the Rivoli, on Queen Street. "I accept that there's another reality," I said, "but you can't seriously believe that you can travel to it via Larry's basement, can you?"

"Why not?" she countered.

"Well, look, these shamans must have cultivated their rituals over years. They probably had apprentices. You can't just go to Mississauga, lie down on a shag rug and meet a power animal. And who are these power animals, anyway? Are they the same thing as angels, or is this a polytheistic religion, or what?"

"As I said," Kate reiterated patiently, "this is the precursor religion, the practice from which all others arose."

"But it's *imaginary*, Kate, come on!"

"Has it ever occurred to you," she retorted, waving a chopstick, "that God speaks to us through our imagination?"

I wasn't convinced. But Kate stuck with shamanism for a while before growing attracted to Buddhism, and then eventually becoming a Quaker. She was still mixing and matching in some ways though, because here we were, ten years later, lying on mats at Yogaspace, a honey-hued room perfumed by scented candles. As we stretched and awaited our instructor, I told her about Don Yancy's NDE, and my cousin shook her heavy auburn tresses and grinned in almost sensual delight, exposing her overlong, rabbity teeth.

"Oh my God," she crowed, "that is extraordinarily cool."

Kate is one of those women who defies the two-dimensional standards of beauty—in magazines and on celluloid—by possessing an allure that is all about movement. Her too-small chin and shapeless nose, her buck teeth and freckles are hidden, gone, irrelevant in the amazing flow of hair, the sly smile, the voluptuous and graceful figure. She was flat out dangerous, I felt, in the Downward Dog pose.

The instructor glided in, hands lightly on her hips, and surveyed the lot of us, some in two-hundred-dollar outfits, others ungainly in T-shirts and sweatpants. She lit candles and turned on a tape of tinkling Tibetan bells. Then, calling us to attention, she reminded us that our feet were rooted in the earth, our spines stretched upward like branches, our abdomens centered, the trunk of life itself. We were a forest of dimly aware religious supplicants in the great spiritual tradition of yogic practice.

"But here's my question," I whispered to Kate, reaching my hands toward my toes. "You know those celebrities who find religion and become Scientologists and Kabbalists and stuff? You would think that faith would lead them to give away some of their fortune to starving people in the Sudan, or work for the churches like Don Yancy, or at least stop worrying about their weight. But it doesn't seem to make any difference. And the other thing is, if they've lost their fear of death, why not blow a head valve on Krispy Kremes and champagne, since they know for certain that the material world doesn't matter?"

Kate simply gazed at me with the unperturbable beneficence of the spiritually aware.

"That's not what it's about," she explained, hunched over in child's pose. "When you realize that you're joined with the universe, you don't have to self-medicate."

"Well, I have to disagree with you about that," I countered, smoothing the curled edge of my mat down. "Didn't shamans argue that drugs are the portal to God? I remember when I did magic mushrooms that summer at Lake Temagami and skipped all our hamburger patties across the lake—do you remember that? I felt very at one with the universe." I crossed my legs and bounced my knees. "Objects no longer had exclusive meaning. Food did not have to be food. The rain wasn't cold. I thought that was quite a spiritual evening. I've always thought that."

Kate shrugged and lunged into warrior pose. "Be still. Then you shall know me as your God."

"What's that from?" I inquired, hanging myself upside down from the waist.

"It's a psalm," answered Kate, flexing her toes.

"Hmm."

We lay down on our mats and closed our eyes, as instructed, although in this case we weren't meant to go off in search of enlightened chipmunks, thank God. The teacher padded back and forth through her field of fallen bodies, waving a stick of burning sage and chanting quietly, "Shanti . . . shanti . . . shanti . . ." This was, inevitably, the time in the few yoga classes I had taken when my mind began to race around. What to make for dinner did I ever pay that gas bill don't forget to fix Lester's jacket zipper why does Calvin have to play hockey on Friday nights I need to return that library book I forgot to call Marina what's wrong with modern poetry maybe I should do a Web search on new treatments for Bernice's cancer if only I knew what kind of cancer she had now that would help I wonder if the Indians in India do as much yoga as we do?

Ommmm, ommmm. Shanti, shanti, shanti.

"Listen, Frannie," Kate said as we rose to leave, "if you're serious about pursuing this subject, you should see my friend Helen."

"Should I?" I rolled up my blue mat and then dropped it, sproing; it unrolled; I rolled it up again. "Why?"

"She's a hypnotherapist. She works with people on relaxation and stress, and I think she can probably get you to that place I'm talking about, where you'll see what I mean about being still."

"She's not going to ask me to make things up," I said, to be sure.

"She'll just lead you like a horse to stillness, and she won't let you think."

25

Got home to find a message from Dana.

Apparently my prayers for Bernice were going unanswered, or conversely, maybe they were answered.

"Calvin," the message ran, "it's Dana. Your mum's not doing too well. Hasn't been eatin' much, not even on Toonie Tuesdays. Shirley's got back from Florida, but she ain't speakin' to Bernice since Bernice accused her of stealin' aa'll her jooolery."

I played this message back twice, unable to believe that Dana would just yack it into the void. Was this not the sort of news one said in person? When Calvin walked in, drumming his fingers on his thighs and feeling particularly pleased with his recording session, I handed him a beer and relayed the message. And then there he was on the phone at the kitchen table, slumped over, resting his forehead in the palm of his hand. An iconic image to me now. My lover on the phone to his relatives in Cape Breton. Sighing, rubbing the space between his eyebrows and talking real low.

"I know she's being paranoid, Shirley," I heard him say, "but she can't help it, she keeps forgetting stuff."

Shirley didn't accept this as a sensible observation requiring a simple acknowledgment. For the next several minutes Calvin was silent, nodding and sighing as she detailed her complaints. I went upstairs to put a *Land Before Time* video on for Lester, then came back down and pulled out a chair, and flipped through the *New Yorker*. There was a profile of Ralph Reed, an evangelical Republican whom Sherman had been enthusing about to me recently. The article quoted Reed's cohort at the Christian Coalition back in 1992: feminism, Pat Robertson had declared, "encourages women to leave their husbands, kill their children, practice witchcraft, destroy capitalism and become lesbians." Did Sherman *read the same English* that I read?

Still getting an earful from Shirley, Calvin plucked at the foil label on his beer bottle and rolled the bits into useless little balls. The kitchen was too bright with the overhead light on, glinting off of our boxy white fridge and our egg-yellow walls. I'd tried to fix up the ambient lighting, make it suitable for conversations with aunts about dying mothers or what have you, but the trouble was simple. The kitchen had no acquaintance with daylight, thanks to Toronto's paranoid fire codes, in which you couldn't punch a window into a wall if that wall stood within yelling distance of your neighbor's wall, lest fire leap through one window, skip across the walkway, and blaze into another window, killing us all. Far better to hunker down inside our safe enclosures than see daylight.

"This is not a cry for help, Shirley, okay? It's not hypochondria, it's not a mistaken diagnosis. I know you've known Mum all your life, and I know she has acted like she was sick when she wasn't. But this is different, it's not a good time to turn your back on her."

I stood up and came behind Calvin, caressing his seal-fur head and massaging his neck. He was, all at once, leaning back into my hands and yet forward, into his resigned discussion with Shirley. He wasn't going to win this, I could tell.

He would have to go out there again.

That isn't such a big deal, is it, for a son to go to his mother? But not all mothers are entirely nice, or wholly present, and not all sons are the only child.

26

It was Valentine's Day when Calvin flew back to Cape Breton, this time indefinitely, with phone numbers for home-care nurses clutched in one hand and his dobro in the other. Ah, romance in midlife. Will that be a candlelit dinner? Or a tense reminder to the one you love that he should check his mother's sneakers for her meds? Lester and I spent the evening with my parents, who presented their grandson with a heart-shaped cake and a brand-new ichthyosaur from Top Banana Toys. What better way to say I love you to this child?

"Can we pack, to go to Heaven?" Lester asked me, perhaps thinking of his father tossing T-shirts in a gym bag, as we walked back home in a light, drifting snow-fall. "Can I bring Orp?" His latest favorite, a saber-toothed tiger with an inexplicable name. "Oh, I don't know about that, hon," I said. *You can't take it with you.*

Tried that line on a five-year-old?

"What does God look like?" Lester asked. "Does he look like a cloud of dust?"

"No, I don't think so, sweetie."

"Well," he persisted, "what do the angels *say* he looks like?" Come on, work with me here, his tone suggested. Help me out, you're the mom.

"I think he's a bright light," I ventured, after a long pause. "I think he's the incarnation of love, maybe more of a feeling than a shape."

"Will I be able to see myself?"

I'd had a few glasses of merlot. I was glad to turn the key in the lock of our home, as if that could end the discussion.

"Oh, don't worry about it, sweetie," I urged, banging my wine-addled head into the door as it swung open. "You have many, many years to grow up before you have to worry about all this."

After he fell asleep, I watched my son in the dim light thrown by his Ikea moon lamp, his helmet hair all mussed and his lashes softly curled against the hollows beneath his eyes. I leaned on the edge of his bunk bed with my hand on his chest and experienced that sharp intake of breath that always meant regret. Les sensed more than he understood, of course, about his father's distress, about that hospital in New Waterford, and his grandmother unable to rise from her bed.

"Turn your eyes to the meadow in its greenness," I wished for him in the silence, "and to the spark of the firefly. Find delight in the scent of autumn and in love, and don't ask me yet about why."

27

On the Friday after Valentine's Day, the *Moral Volcano* sponsored a cocktail party at the Toronto Press Club, a stodgy old gentlemen's venue of yore, near Hy's Steakhouse downtown. The plan, according to Hilary, who popped her head into our office to invite us, was for everyone to imbibe sufficient quantities of liquor, after which four witty gentlemen would engage in an entertaining debate. "Be it resolved," Hilary said, her eyes sparkling in anticipation, "money can't buy you love."

"Oh, that sounds like fun," I said. Avery and Goran barely looked up from their desks. But I was curious. We used to have debates like that in university. Everyone would show up half-corked on cheap beer, and then heckle and applaud as the class clowns assumed the challenge of arguing a cliché.

Hilary and Sherman were particularly excited about their event because a famous conservative from England named Boris Something had come to Toronto to promote his new book, *I Eat Liberals for Lunch*, and had agreed to take part in the debate for a lark—a bit of decompression after a whirlwind day of interviews and lectures.

After much threatening and cajoling, I persuaded Avery to come with me. "Don't you want to hear Boris Something?" I argued. "He's famous in England."

"No," said Avery, "I don't, really. But if Calvin's away and you don't want to go unaccompanied . . ." He looked at me dubiously.

"It's a scene," I said. "It could be interesting."

Avery shrugged. "I'll do it, for you."

"Remind me what scene you were expecting," he said, when we arrived at the appointed time a few nights later after dropping Lester off at my mom's. Several of the attendees were huddled on the snowy front steps of the club smoking cigarettes and trading quips about tax law as they pulled their black overcoats tight against the wind. They waved us through their midst in good cheer; everyone seemed up for a party. The club inside was packed with chattering pundits and businessfolk.

"Okay, maybe I was imagining a different scene," I allowed, recalling the art opening and fancy soirees I sometimes attended in New York. I had forgotten that people interested mainly in politics, on the left or on the right, tended to shout "Hear, hear" instead of shaking their booty to Sean Paul.

"Frannie!" called out Sherman, sailing over to hold me lightly by the shoulders, his face beaming. "I'm so glad you could come!"

"My pleasure," I said, pleased to be welcomed, and hoping that he would say hello to Avery.

"We have a very special guest tonight," confided Sherman, leaning into me and ignoring Avery. "Boris Johnson! From London's *Spectator*! He's going to be one of the debaters."

Just then, an imposing man in a gold tie, clasping a BlackBerry, came up and grabbed Sherman's wrist, and after a flurry of excuse me's and gracious nods we were left to our own devices.

To assign myself a purpose as Avery got rid of our coats, I headed for the bar, wending my way through a sea of bright-eyed and dark-suited men, with the occasional splash of color signifying a female. By the time I'd reached the linen-covered table with the booze, I'd done a rough calculation and come up with a ratio of three females to ten males a square yard. "Why aren't there more women here?" I asked Avery, when he caught up with me.

"Maybe there aren't enough female neo-cons to fill a room," he speculated.

"Can I have white wine?" I asked the bartender, a dark-haired and almond-eyed man whose musculature threatened to pop the button of his white jacket. I offered him a flirtatious smile, if only because he was the sole man in the room who gave off an air of sexuality instead of nerdy glee.

171

"Oh! Please! Don't even get me started on energy futures!" proclaimed the fellow behind us, chuckling at his friend.

"No, I'm serious," the friend protested amiably, "just give me a quick rundown on the numbers."

"So what are you going to propose?" another fellow asked a man who looked—I was fascinated to note—exactly like Peter on *Family Guy*, "Can money buy you love?"

"I'm gonna argue that money can buy you *time*," Peter answered with a grin, "which you need, while you wait for your lady to make up her friggin' mind."

"Frannie!"

There are some voices you never forget. Particularly the one belonging to the brother who hung you out the window by the ankles when you were ten.

"David," I replied, knocking back half of my glass in two gulps as I watched him wend his way toward us. "How you doing?"

My brother, resplendent in a gleaming red tie, gave me a one-handed hug and waved over his wife, Penny, with the other.

"Look what the tide washed up," he remarked happily.

David always seemed delighted to run into me. It was odd, though, that he had to run into me to ever see me at all. A curious "I love you, get lost" sort of vibe was at work there. My sister-in-law, on the other hand, approached me as if I were cat vomit. Oh for God's sake, another wet pile of hair on the carpet. David, can you please deal with this?

"Hi," Penny said, her shoulders tense within the cranberry cashmere turtleneck she wore over a black crepe skirt. She kept her hands clasped at her waist, unwilling to touch me. Her platinum blond hair, bobbed so that it curved inward at her piquant chin, barely moved as she nodded hello.

"Hi, Penny," I said, "how's it going?"

"Great," she replied, and gave me a toothy smile that reminded me of a chimp's grin. Thanks to Lester's nature shows, I'd learned that a primate grin served as a warning to other primates to fuck off right this minute.

"Hello, I'm Avery Dellaire," said Avery, shooting out his hand for Penny to shake, trying to act as a diversion and make everyone feel pleasant again.

David took the cue and began chatting with Avery about books, explaining who Avery was to Penny, while I stood back, still unnerved. Relations between me and Penny had soured since Lester was born. I know it was my fault. I'd been housesitting for her and David while they went to England, and Calvin and I had made a bit of a mess. But usually you hope to get over these things in a family, let the water go under the bridge, once you've paid to replace the Belgian linen hand towels that you used as diapers and that sort of thing.

It just hadn't worked with Penny. I couldn't do the alchemy with her wherein kindness and a simple "I'm sorry" were transformed into the gift of strengthened friendship. When the conversation petered out between Avery and David we all moved on—the two of them latching onto the famous Boris, who had just swished past, while Avery and I scanned the crowd to no avail and felt self-conscious. I suddenly wished I could talk to Father McPhee. I wanted to be back there in that empty hospital room in the sunlight, conversing with somebody who welcomed what was truly on my mind. I didn't want to be in a room crowded with black-suited magpies, attracted to glittery words. I didn't need people who were clever, I needed someone who was wise.

28

"You're stressed," observed Helen, leading me into one of her session rooms at the Oasis Hypnosis Clinic on Yonge Street. Was that the first thing she said to all of her clients? I followed her out of the clinic's soft-cushioned waiting room with its soothing framed seascapes. She walked ahead of me down the hall with a polished stride, her shoulders erect and her hips swaying, attired crisply in a chocolate-brown jacket and matching skirt. Her silvery-blond hair looked as solid as a mannequin's wig. I remembered that Kate had described her as a former management consultant.

We reached a softly lit room filled with flowers, and she gestured me toward a fat leather armchair that proved impossible to sit up straight in. As soon as I leaned back in the buttery leather, I reclined like a splayed baby.

Helen herself sat lightly on a swivel chair beside a mahogany escritoire that held a cassette player and a notebook.

"Why are you stressed?" Helen asked, fixing me with huge brown eyes, dark as espresso.

"Oh," I shrugged, trying to raise my head out of folds of black leather. "I'm not. You know. I'm fine. My mother-in-law is dying, and I worry about Iraq. But who doesn't? And global warming, which I would like to see one single solitary politician somewhere this side of Pluto pay attention to before it's too late and my son finds himself abandoned by civilization as we know it and scrounging for snails. But that's just the same old same old. I'm not particularly stressed."

Helen nodded, smiling serenely. "Every issue is manageable if you have good techniques for managing your feelings about it. Hypnosis is a technique. There's no magic to it, no swinging pocket watch." She gave a merry little snort. "It's just a way to calm yourself down and focus your attention on your feelings, and then allow them to flow evenly, rather than getting knotted up in the chest. Does your chest hurt?"

She knew it did. I nodded, from somewhere deep within the chair. I felt as if I were a lost comb.

"Alright, then," said Helen, sitting back, "I want you to close your eyes and relax." She clicked on her cassette player, and the small cool room filled with ocean sounds. Helen lowered her voice to merge in pitch and rhythm with the waves, and guided me through a visualization sequence involving a beach. It's interesting that everyone associates ultimate relaxation with being by the sea. I wonder if people who live on the coast all the time are more relaxed than everyone else, and can barely get off their backs, or whether they have a different imaging sequence. Do they imagine lying in a richly upholstered chair in an affluent city where they can actually afford someone like Helen . . . ?

"Now," she said softly, "I want you to go back to the first time you felt this feeling of stress and anxiety, the very first time."

I lay there like a felled tree, utterly immobilized, but my mind obediently began to stagger around in search of suitable memories. Eventually, all I could come up with was being afraid of the dark in grade four.

"Gooood," Helen said, soothing, when I raised my pinkie as she had instructed, to show that I'd remembered . . . well, that. Enough. Indeed, I had remembered lying in my little bed with its Winnie the Pooh quilt, listening to my little battery-operated radio that was perched on the windowsill, even as I felt scared witless of the staircase outside my door. "Sunshine on my shoulders makes me happy," warbled John Denver, and I loved him so much, he took the edge off my terrified suspicion that there was a monster on those stairs, possibly a serial killer, like the so-called Hillside Stranglers of Los Angeles, whose murders of young women were then in the news. Every night that year, in grade four, it all hung in the balance between my enjoyment of how sunshine felt on my shoulders, and my growing awareness of news. News went well beyond fairy-tale monsters and introduced me to actual terrors that my parents could not dismiss. I fought for balance every night for a while there, between ignoring monsters and fearing men as those stairs loomed and shifted in the shadows.

Helen, feeling satisfied by the raising of my finger, instructed me to go on and revisit all of my memories of anxiety, one by one, and to cleanse them by re-envisioning each event as a positive experience. Oh, sure. I could not, of course, begin to remember every preposterous fear I had ever had in my life, it would be like trying to recall the number of bananas I'd eaten. But still, relaxed and captive in her chair, I tried. I did. My brain cells fired sluggishly. I hit on the time I went camping in Big Bend and was mortally fearful of mountain lions. Then, *ping*, the choice moment when I realized that I was pregnant with Calvin's baby. The night, in grade eleven, that I heard on TV that the Soviets had invaded Afghanistan. The time I couldn't board a plane without the prospect of losing control of my bladder. The night Bernice and I played bingo and I won.

Finally, I gave up, and just listened to the ambient noise outside on Yonge Street. A car drove by, blasting Avril Lavigne. After a while, I realized that I was supposed to have raised my finger, to indicate to Helen that I'd completed the archival work. Done! Remembered every bloody thing that ever undid me, and with miraculous swiftness, too! I gave her the signal, and at once, Helen dispatched me to my earliest memory of life. I thought about it, and decided that it was disembarking from an airplane on a holiday to Mexico at the age of . . .

four? Brown faces. Heat rising visibly and surprisingly off the pavement. The novel fragrance of the sea. I raised a pinkie.

Encouraged, she pushed on. "Now you are two years old . . ."

Had I not run headlong into the limit of recollection? But she urged me to visualize myself at two, then at one, and still younger and younger until there I was, she announced, to my surprise and her evident pleasure, in my mother's womb.

"You are in a velvety, enveloping darkness," she intoned, in her marvelous, mellifluous voice.

Oh, boy. I was keen to agree with her. I loved her voice, and the idea of where she was coaxing me, but really I had to concede that I wasn't inside my mother by any stretch of the imagination. I simply wasn't. It was a terrible thing to say, I sensed, but I felt very strongly that I was sitting in a chair at the Oasis Hypnosis Clinic.

Before raising my objections, though, I considered my options, for I felt deeply comfortable there, with my mouth hanging slightly open, even drooling a bit, and I decided, you know what? Okay! Spirituality demands the suspension of empirical knowledge. It calls out to the imagination, to gnosis, to the self as experienced without objective proof. An appropriate pause elapsed, dully respectful of a fully grown woman finding herself in her mother's long-forgotten womb. And another waved pinkie, this time feeling distinctly untruthful.

Next stop: a blue mist. Helen described it to me, and said I was to feel "peaceful and content," yet, "something is missing, a challenge," some ineffable sense impelling me back in time into . . . my previous life!

"Your feet have landed on the ground," Helen said. "I want you to look down, and tell me what you see. What are you wearing on your feet?"

On my feet? Like, right now? Oh, God! I'm still thinking about the blue mist, whether it would be a dry ice effect, or what. I struggled to imagine my feet, and decided, lamely, I felt, that I was wearing a pair of sandals.

"Can you describe the sandals?"

Pause. "They have multiple straps."

"Look up from your feet. What are you wearing on your body?"

I had no idea. I couldn't see my body. All I could see was the inside of my eyelids. It felt wrong to baldly make things up.

"Look around you," Helen prodded. "Can you describe where you are?" I pictured a lake surrounded by dense forest. "Northern Europe," I told her, without confidence.

She asked me to go to where there were people. I visualized a tavern. "Who is with you?" No one. I was hesitant to populate it with the characters from *Shakespeare in Love*, whence the tavern image came.

"Leave the tavern," Helen said. "Try to find a mode of transportation." I ducked out of the tavern, and for some reason all I could see on the street was a foot-propelled scooter.

I suddenly felt the need to guffaw, but successfully suppressed it.

Undaunted, she sent me elsewhere. I envisioned a table outside on a hilltop, overlooking a lush valley. The vista looked suspiciously like the one I had seen on a holiday to Tuscany.

Helen forwarded me to the moment of my death and asked me to describe it. For someone so adept at imagining that precise thing, you'd think I'd come up with quite the scenario. But I was too relaxed to lie. And the truth was that I sensed nothing but a streetcar rattling by outside on St. Clair Avenue. A few minutes later, a phone rang somewhere. After that, I heard the swish of silk as Helen crossed her legs. The insides of my eyelids remained dark.

"I'm blind," I suggested.

"Go on," she prodded.

"And deaf."

She sighed.

"All right, then," she asked. "What are the lessons you learned in this lifetime?"

Er . . . ah . . . oh come on, Helen, don't do this to me.

It's not healthy to live your life as a static tableau with no people in it?

You are what you wear on your feet?

Love is blind?

We headed back into the blue mist.

"Maybe I didn't have any other lives," I told Calvin when I got home and called him in Cape Breton, before running back out to fetch Lester from daycare.

"Maybe you were a plant," he suggested.

Hindus would have thought of that.

"Calvin, are you smoking?" I asked, for I heard him exhale.

"Yes, I am."

"Why?"

Calvin hadn't smoked in years. Well, he smoked pot, of course, but never in houses or on phones. Usually just in the alley behind bars when he was waiting to hear or play music.

"I'm smoking because I want to knock five years off my life so that I never have to wear a pair of Depends."

"Oh, come on." I pulled off my socks and eased under the comforter in our bed. Cradled the phone and closed my eyes.

"And if that doesn't work, Frannie, then as soon as I hit eighty, I want you to shoot me in the back of the head. I never want to piss myself, and I never want to forget where I put my drum kit. And let me tell you this, if I can't remember who Lester Bangs is *earlier* than eighty, then you have to shoot me then."

"I'm not going to shoot you—"

"Lemme finish. I see absolutely no redeeming fucking point to being too old to hold my water or follow the plot of a TV sitcom. Because you know what? I've been a baby. Been there, done that."

"You've been drinking, haven't you?" I asked, more curious than indignant. Calvin liked his beer, but usually in modest quantities. Rarely did I catch the slur I was hearing tonight in his speech.

"Yes, I have! Me, Dana and a pitcher at the Room with

a Cue. And if I develop liver disease, I will send out my own fucking party invitations. You know why? Because I'd rather go down in my prime than waddle around in diapers blubbering about swollen legs and stolen rugs."

"But that doesn't have to happen," I argued, more or less for the sake of argument, since I understood perfectly what he meant. "Look at Picasso, or Dr. Richardson."

"Nobody but Picasso gets to be Picasso, and Richardson's a freak, a weird, battery-operated antique. How useful has he been? I can't even find him and I've been in this godforsaken place for a week now."

"It's not about being useful, Cal."

"No?" he bellowed. "What's it about then? Living just to go on living? What's the purpose of that? Tell me, Frannie, tell me. You can't swing a fucking cat these days without hitting another headline about oatmeal adding two years to your life. It's all this dumb-assed tally of years. Years doing what, Frannie? What do you want three point six more years for, if you're going to spend them sucking air out of oxygen masks and repeating your anecdotes?"

I sighed. "If it helps, Goran says to hell with a long life if you can't smoke Camels."

Calvin remained silent.

"You there . . . ?" I ventured.

"My mother overdosed on some medicine they gave her today to control her swelling, and started hallucinating. She thought she was being chased by bears. She was screaming, Frannie, and there wasn't a bloody thing I could do."

"Oh, God."

"What is the purpose of this?" he asked at length, his voice breaking. "What's the point?"

"She has you," I answered. "Isn't that something? She has you with her, and your dad waiting for her, and you just have to lead her on through."

"Oh, man," whispered Calvin, and he sounded so broken, I wanted to wrap my arms around him and make him whole. "I don't know, Frannie, I don't know."

29

"Did I ever tell you about how Tolstoy nearly killed himself when he was fifty?"

Of course Avery is going to ask me this kind of question on a Monday morning.

"No, you never told me about how Tolstoy nearly killed himself when he was fifty."

Avery launches into discourses on nineteenth-century writers the way other people begin jokes by saying, "A man walked into a bar."

"So, Tolstoy was famous at that point," he went on. "Married to the love of his life. Abundant children. Vast estates. Uhhhh. But he was, I gather, suddenly overwhelmed by a sense of meaninglessness. I think he said something like . . . uhhh . . . 'Well, I'm as famous as Gogol, now, and Molière and even Shakespeare. So what?'"

"What did he mean, so what?" We were in our familiar dinner-table positions, gazing back and forth across six feet of space.

"He meant there was no meaning. So, so what? If life had no meaning, beyond what was really, essentially reducible to physical reproduction, then all he was doing was a fancier variety of a fruit-fly dance."

"Oh." That was interesting. Calvin should've been there—he'd have cheered right up.

"Once he had that insight, then he couldn't go on deluding himself that anything he did was important, and there was nothing for it but to kill himself."

"Did you hear about this on *The Oprah Winfrey Show*?" I wondered.

"What do you mean?"

"Never mind."

"Okay, no, let me read it to you. I've got it here on the shelf." Avery found the book he wanted and spent some time flipping the pages until he put up a hand, as if to silence me, and read aloud:

"'My position was terrible. I knew that I could find nothing in the way of rational knowledge except a denial of life; and in faith I could find nothing except a denial of reason, and this was even more impossible than a denial of life. . . . According to faith, it followed that in order to understand the meaning of life I would have to turn away from reason, the very thing for which meaning was necessary.'"

Avery paused, and twisted his arms, fixing me with a searching stare. I stared back, blank. So he moved ahead in the text, and finished with:

"'Faith is the knowledge of the meaning of human life, whereby the individual does not destroy himself but lives. Faith is the force of life. If a man lives, then he must have faith in something.'"

Avery looked at me expectantly. I took a deep breath, and then inhaled. I took another deep breath and inhaled again. "Okay, this is good." I returned his gaze, smiling. "This is way better than what Job said. I think I can actually turn this over in my mind."

To that end, I sat at my desk with the passage from Tolstoy that Avery had read aloud, and read and reread it for an hour and a half, trying to make sure that I was square with what he meant. Did Oprah go through this, I wondered, when she announced she wanted *Anna Karenina* for her book club, or was it just mothers like me, caught between Avery-ness and Lester-ness and Calvin-ness who felt like they were studying a bingo sheet and trying to figure out where to stamp the bits they recognized before time ran out.

30

"Momma, what are you doing?"

"You shouldn't be awake, honey. Why are you out of bed?" I clutched the red pencil I'd been using to edit O'Sullivan's column more tightly, annoyed by the sudden interruption. Lester failed to sense my mood and climbed onto the futon couch beside me.

"I had a bad dream," he said.

"Like what, sweetie, what did you dream?" I pulled him closer.

"I dreamed that Daddy turned into a tin can."

"A can?"

He nodded, and bent his head to my chest. I smoothed his hair and stifled the urge to run screaming into the street in my pajamas, beating my chest and demanding to know why no one ever made any sense. Instead, I gave him a kiss and recommended bedrest as the best recovery from dreams of shocking transformation. "Just lie down and think of good things," I suggested. "Imagine eating an ice cream sundae on the beach." He wiggled off the couch resignedly and padded back upstairs.

I returned to my work, which was giving me a headache. The column that O'Sullivan had written this week was about gay marriage: how "weak politicians quailed" in the wind of "whiners' rights" and invariably capitulated to every impetuous human demand. Marriage was a "sacred union" between a man and a woman, and nothing in scripture allowed otherwise. Was there any point, I wondered tiredly, to reminding O'Sullivan that marriage was a civil contract that had nothing to do with the Church until the eighteenth century? The lower classes used to jump over broomsticks to cement their bond. Actually, if I felt that he was interested in genuine argument, I might be excited to point out the historical context of marriage. But by now I had realized that O'Sullivan was merely enamored of rhetoric. This was just "be it resolved" with a cocktail in a written form.

What had I been thinking, agreeing to edit the man? I suppose I hadn't ever read through the *Volcano* before taking the gig, but I ought to have known. I started reading his stuff aloud to Avery to see if I could enlist his assistance—the two of us marveling that it had this surface flair, this ability to use nouns and verbs in the same sentences and to pull off pleasing metaphors, but it wasn't written in Human.

"There are always going to be certain genres," Avery

said a couple of weeks ago, as we sat at Nate's Diner on Spadina Avenue around the corner from the office, "art catalogs, for instance, that cannot be accused of being written in English, without successfully defending the charges. But O'Sullivan's trouble seems different."

"How so?" I asked, smoothing sour cream over my perogies.

"Maybe it's just me," Avery mused, "but I tend to think of human rants as having a fairly predictable overlay of delivery and content. Uhhh . . . I mean, a traceable connection between emotion and style." He shot one arm out and scratched it absentmindedly. "Consider, for example, the statement 'Fuck you, I hate you fucking fuckers.' Nine times out of ten, this statement will be shouted, snarled or—in writing—scribbled with many words in italics ending in exclamation marks. Right?"

I nodded, and washed down my perogies with a nutritious sip of Sprite.

"Sometimes, depending upon the rant, an object will be thrown . . . uhhh . . . or dishes swept from a table. A door slammed. A column completed in CAPITAL LETTERS. In any event," Avery bent over to take a slurp of his soup, "the wellspring of emotion will be clearly in evidence. But this is not the case with Sherman. He is able to write, in essence, 'Fuck you, I hate you fucking fuckers' with an air of cool detachment, as if he were an economist musing on the prospects for third-quarter recession."

"But his emotional content twists off within the first few sentences," I joined in, "and then you find yourself

191

following an increasingly bizarre trajectory of deeply felt hostility toward the French."

"Exactly," said Avery, "like that time last year when he called the French 'cheese-eating surrender monkeys.'"

We both fell silent for a time, concentrating on our lunches.

"Maybe he was given up for adoption by a French mother," Avery concluded, pushing away his empty bowl and tossing in the crumpled napkin.

"That's possible," I reflected. "My mother says you cannot know a man until you see him *en famille.*"

31

As it happened, I had a chance to see O'Sullivan *en famille* a short while later, but it turned out to be the incorrect *famille*. Or, more properly phrased, the illicit *famille* that he would just as soon not have introduced to me.

This unexpected encounter came about due to Lester's newfound interest in five-pin bowling. He had recently attended a birthday party that took place at a bowling alley, and now it was the thing to do instead of watch TV. Go to the Dufferin Mall lanes, spend an inordinate amount of time trying on ill-fitting bowling shoes, purchase nachos with Cheez Whiz, and then wing ball after ball a full two feet down the lane, thence to dribble into the gutter and stall out about halfway toward the never-struck pins. It was fun. This is what the pair of us happened to be engaged in one Saturday afternoon when I noticed, to my utter astonishment, O'Sullivan sitting on an orange plastic chair two lanes over and feverishly nuzzling a woman's slender neck. She was pretty, with her dark hair pinned up, and she was more or less ignoring him as she offered up words of encouragement to their daughter, a plump girl of twelve or so who was clearly very keen on her game.

"How odd," I thought. I had never imagined Sherman doing something as plebeian and PG-rated as hanging out at the Dufferin lanes. I watched him with his family for a while, and then en route to the concession stand for a refill of nachos, I took Lester by the hand and ducked down to lane six to introduce myself.

"Frannie!" O'Sullivan cried out in mortal terror. "What are you doing here?"

I hesitated, thrown off stride by his anxiety. His Gerber-baby eyes were as wide and frightened and fixed on me as if I were holding aloft a hissing grenade. Reflexively, I looked down at myself. "What's wrong?" I asked. When he didn't reply, I gabbled into the ensuing silence, punctuated as it was by bowling balls crashing into pins. "I'm sorry, I didn't mean to disturb you, I just thought I'd introduce you to my son and—you know—say hello to Cheryl." I looked at his wife, hoping that she'd smile.

Cheryl, who had risen and now stood with her arms crossed tightly against her low-cut black T-shirt, regarded me angrily. "My name isn't Cheryl," she said, glancing pointedly at Sherman, as if this were the very essence of all arguments they'd ever had. "His wife's name is Cheryl."

"Oh!" I exclaimed as Lester tugged on my arm, unwilling to be interrupted in his pursuit of nachos by an unfathomable conversation. "I'm sorry. I just—it's nice to meet you . . ."

"Gail," she offered tersely.

"Gail," I echoed. "Well, I work with Sherman, anyway, so I just wanted to say hi."

At that, I turned tail and followed Lester to the snack stand.

O'Sullivan caught up to me in the staircase at work in the following week.

"Frannie," he ventured, skipping up the steps and then pressing his fingers into my forearm to halt me. "What you saw—she's an old friend of mine."

"Right," I said lightly, refusing to look at him. I didn't want to know, I didn't care.

"It would be wrong of you," he added, as I attempted to politely pull my arm away, "to draw salacious conclusions from what you saw."

Oh, how strange, this was going to be about *my* moral judgment? "Forget about it, Sherman," I muttered as he let his hand drop, "we have nothing to discuss."

"No," he said, easing into a grin, "of course not. That is the point."

32

Sherman O'Sullivan reminded me of my uncle Svend. It took me a while to figure out the similarity, given that Svend was a neuropsychiatrist who paid scant attention to politics and didn't bother to be charming. He was obsessed by his science, and spent endless hours in a laboratory at Toronto's Western Hospital on the fringes of Chinatown. I didn't imagine he paid much attention to his workplace community at the corner of Dundas and Bathurst Street, which featured a McDonald's staffed by South Asian immigrants who handed out biscuits, as per the company's dog-friendly policy, at the drive-through, while bellowing: "You need dog food?" Nor the Scadding Court Community Centre, which sometimes filled their swimming pool with trout and had a fishing day, or Kim Bo Restaurant, the Balloon King and the Chinese grocery fronted by crates of withered bok choy.

Svend zoomed back and forth in his polished Lexus from the hospital's underground garage to his home in Rosedale, wholly unconcerned with the intervening world.

Lately, he had been experimenting with what he called the God Helmet, a canary-yellow hard hat that he'd outfitted with electrical wires. According to my mother, who followed his academic papers, Svend had devised a method for electrifying the brain's frontal lobe in such a way that it could induce mystic visions, thus invalidating all spiritual epiphanies throughout the millennia of human experience and chalking them up, instead, to random electromagnetic perturbances. To go about this business of neatly erasing the insights of the prophets, Svend employed unwitting subjects from the University of Toronto, who strolled into his lab in faux Beatles haircuts, listening to Outkast on their iPods. After an hour-long session in the helmet, they staggered out and walked, elated and unseeing onto Dundas, en route to amazed proclamations to their friends about being in the presence of God.

Svend wrote them up as case reports for conferences he attended on neurotheology. Religious belief is all in the mind, Svend and his neurotheology colleagues told one another, sipping coffee from paper cups in far-flung hotels buzzing with brainy excitement. These researchers were disciples of Darwin and devout followers of evolutionary psychology, who deemed faith an evolutionary adaptation of early hominids. God enabled humans to cope with consciousness without going mad. How this worked was unclear to me. I suppose the branches of hominid that hadn't developed the God gene drove themselves crazy with death anxiety and eventually all cut off their ears like Van Gogh, or committed mass suicide. Who could know?

My cousin Kate denounced her father's work as a venal attempt to justify his leaving Aunt Mary and her, by proving that there was no immutable standard of ethics. Without a God, there needn't be guilt, except where it was convenient for cooperative survival. Kate called this the "sociopath's creed." My father, who was Mary's older brother, tended to agree with her. But I wasn't sure. After puzzling over O'Sullivan's weird fear of liberals, I got to thinking that Svend was mostly driven to condemn sentiments that struck him as disorderly because of his own fear of chaos. He was always on the brink of flying out of control. He'd had two marriages, numerous affairs and a long bout with alcoholism. He drove way too fast, and had a volatile temper. Like O'Sullivan, he loathed ambiguities, and perhaps it all boiled down to a need for control. The world was a chaotic cosmos filled with tempests and temptation, and science, in Svend's case—or absolutes, when it came to O'Sullivan—served as the best method of containment. A lid for Pandora's box.

I was never certain which came first, Uncle Svend's control-freak personality, or his impulse for excess. All I knew was that, for a man devoted to order, he had a marked habit of fostering discord every time he got up in the morning. He was, for instance, a legend in the family for holding parties that began with light chatter and anecdotes and ended with objects being hurled across the room.

I almost missed Kate's birthday party (case in point) because Calvin was still in New Waterford and Lester had come down with the flu. At the last minute my father, who preferred books and comfortable couches to predictably histrionic dinners at Svend's, offered to babysit for me. He wanted to show Lester his new collection of Curious George books, republished with all of the original illustrations.

Thus freed, I bought Kate a copy of *Chicken Soup for the Deeply Offended Daughter's Soul*, and drove off to Rosedale, a grossly affluent and intriguingly maze-like neighborhood filled with mansions concealed behind maple trees. I don't know why, but it isn't possible to travel a single street in Rosedale for more than three blocks without somehow arriving back at where you began, having been fooled by the street's subtle arcing. You cannot reach your destination without getting lost at least four times—it's like a poor person's baffle. Only residents of Rosedale, and outsiders with supreme determination, ever manage to prevail.

Svend inhabited an austere, ivy-covered brick house, which he shared with his third wife, Rose, the daughter of a liquor scion whose fortune will secure Svend's retirement fantasy of being one of the first private citizens to rocket to the moon. The trade-off, as my mother pointed out, was that Rose was a questionable candidate for the title of domestic goddess, ill-suited to a man who stored everything in neat containers. Rose loved entertaining, but she didn't much care for sweeping, and she fancied herself an artist who liked to work with felt and human hair, which made her house look like a rodent's nest. She also had a flock of insane Pomeranians, who lent an interesting ambience to the household. Between the canine hysteria and the human hair, it was difficult to figure out how Svend had fallen so in love with Rose that he could actually dwell on the premises. But that's the funny thing about love, isn't it? Sometimes the heart wants what the mind cannot abide.

I liked Rose. Personally. I thought she was very warm, always curious and graciously self-effacing. Kate despised her, and rarely accepted an invitation to Rose and Svend's house for dinner. But this year, Aunt Mary had encouraged Kate to go.

"Just go, *go!* He's your father," urged Mary, a practical woman who got over Svend's departure far more swiftly than her daughter.

I parked my car behind the Toyota SUV my brother owned, which had sparked several arguments between us, with me favoring the environment and him favoring his wife Penny's phobia of dying in a car accident. As I entered the house, the Pomeranians swarmed around my feet, barking and trying to herd me back out the door as if I were a serial killer with a chainsaw.

"Stop," urged Rose, shooing at the dogs mildly with her hand. As always, she had parted her thick auburn hair far to the left, so that a curtain of tresses fell down the right side of her face, hiding the scars she'd incurred a few years ago when she fell off her bike into the gravel of the driveway. She was so clever and consistent about this hairdo that I had only ever seen her left eye.

My brother David was in the drawing room, nursing a bourbon as he reclined in a wingback chair, leg crossed and foot swinging in the air. "I haven't seen *The Passion of the Christ* yet," he was saying, his lips drawn into a smirk, "but I'm certainly enjoying the drink of the house. How was the day of the sister? Still concerned about the illness of the son?"

I smiled. It was odd, I thought, that Penny wasn't here. Had she and David had a fight?

"Frances's more abiding concern is the sickness of the mother-in-law, David," observed my own mother, seated in a love seat next to Rose, clutching her gin and tonic and gazing disapprovingly at her son.

"Oh dear," said Rose, reaching her arms up to me, "I'm sorry to hear that, Frannie. I hadn't heard that Calvin's mother was sick. Would you like a scotch?"

I sat down in the wing chair that matched my brother's and smoothed out my skirt, now smeared with pawprints. "I'm okay, Rose, thanks."

"Rough about the mother-in-law," offered David, in the gruff, game tone of someone consoling a friend from a losing city about the hockey playoffs. "So is she toast, or can they treat her?"

"Those are the options?" asked Kate, suddenly aroused from her sullen position in the corner of the room beside a square of human hair mounted on a chrome pipe. "Death or repair, like a broken car?" Kate sounded mocking. She never had liked my brother. "What about how she's feeling emotionally and spiritually, David?"

"Okay, okay." My brother genuflected toward Kate. "Beware of the wrath of the cousin. I know all about spiritual treatment. Penny's down in Baja with her mum. They're both having out-of-body experiences on the beach to treat their depressions."

Was Penny still depressed about being infertile, I wondered, or had something else laid her low?

"Well," piped up Rose, hoping to change the subject, "we went to see *The Passion of the Christ,* and one thing that really jumped out at me is that Jesus appears to have invented the dinette set."

Everyone stared at Rose. The Pomeranians snuffled and panted, out of synch with Ella Fitzgerald, who sang on the CD player.

"I don't know what historical sources Mel Gibson was basing his sets on," Rose continued, adjusting the sleeves of her gray silk shirt, "but there's a scene in the film where Jesus shows his mother how he's made a table. For all the world, it's a dinette set. It's interesting, I think, that he was a carpenter, and yet that is never talked about in the Bible."

The force of Kate's eye-roll almost threw her off balance. "I believe the film was attempting to portray Jesus's suffering, not his furniture design."

"Well, you have a point there," said David, raising his bourbon as if in toast. His tone was poised on the knife's edge between flippant and sincere. Slick, rich guy in that soft Italian wool suit and subdued gold tie. Always juuuust—have I imagined it?—on the verge of bursting out laughing.

"Well, for Heaven's sake," said my mother, "I don't know why this Mel Gibson is taking everything so seriously, after making his fortune in dog comedies."

"In what, Mum?" I asked.

"In that series of movies," she replied, swishing the ice in her drink, "*Bad Max*, or what have you."

Purposefully or not, and one could never tell with my mother, she had defused the tension, for Kate, Rose, David and I all had to laugh.

"Dinner!" announced Svend, blowing into the room with his arms spread wide. He was very tall, and commanded people through sheer height. His outfit was less charismatic, as he wore navy-blue dress pants hemmed too short, with red sports socks and Adidas. Apparently, this was Yard Work Wear, which doubled in a pinch as Birthday Dinner Fashion. Knowing Svend, he'd just completely lost track of time out there in the backyard, unwrapping the burlap from his bushes.

We filed into the dining room, whose walls—painted aubergine—were covered in framed collages. Each one had a little card beneath noting the title and materials, the way they do at art galleries. "*Autumn Tempest*. Shredded wool on baseboard." Or: "*Artist Self-portrait*. Hair, felt and tinsel on drawer-lining paper." I couldn't entirely see the resemblance to Rose, but I suppose it was meant to be more a reflection of her self-image than what she actually looked like.

Chairs scraped out, glasses clinked, and David saw fit to toss out one more comment about *The Passion of the Christ.*

"Really, I just want to add about that Gibson movie, that it blows my mind how many people willingly file into theaters to sit through violence just because it's got Christ's stamp of approval."

"Well, nobody knows what Jesus would have thought of it," I said.

"He sure ain't gonna turn down the new converts it brings," retorted David, with that pseudo-folksy sarcasm of his.

"Religious belief is a cognitive virus," Svend offered cheerfully as Rose handed him a plate of peas and ham and gestured at the silver serving bowl she'd managed to fill with less than a cup of mashed potatoes for all present. More scotch?

"What do you mean it's a cognitive virus? That is a totally asinine statement," said Kate, narrowing her eyes at her father. "You're so in denial."

"Well, that's—I don't find that a fair statement, Katie," Svend responded, hunkering down to his spartan dinner. "I think we can agree that religion has ignited more wars than not, created more harm than good."

Kate grew as tense as a leopard about to pounce across the table. "You are so stunningly shallow on this subject," she growled. "What about Mother Teresa, and Jean Vanier, and Ignatius Loyola and . . . and . . . there has just been case after case of a spiritual person ennobled to do good, to set the example that everyone has followed, in how to care for the poor, and for animals, and how to be kind and judicious, and it's just so bloody convenient for you to dismiss them as having some virus, and then focus on how religion drives war."

David, nursing his fourth bourbon, if I'd counted correctly—and now I was really wondering what had depressed Penny—interrupted before Svend could reply. "Okay, okay," he said. "Hold it for a second, Kate. Let's try to understand what everybody's talking about. Svend, I've never quite got what your argument is. Basically, it sounds like you're saying, never mind St. Augustine and Mohammed, and Christ and like, Tolstoy and Confucius and Buddha and their yackety-yack. The deal went down like this. Over our five million years of brain development as a species, at some point, for no particular reason, a mutant gene within an ape's brain enabled that particular ape to believe fanciful shit that was wholly unanchored in the observable facts."

Svend nodded and David nodded back, then took a fueling sip of bourbon. "So, this mutation led to a particular species of deluded ape that eventually triumphed over all of the other, more pragmatic apes, who did not believe in fanciful shit, because the deluded ape didn't care if he died, and all the other apes did. Like, if he got eaten by a lion, so what? There was an afterlife. Cool. Meanwhile, the pragmatic apes were busy saving their butts, and yet they didn't survive."

David stabbed a pea with his fork, lifted it to his mouth, chewed contemplatively. "Instead, the fanciful and deluded apes managed to promote their genes, because they were more able to adapt to the fact that a sabre-toothed tiger was about to crack open their skulls for a snack, and *c'est la vie*. It's God's will. Is that it? "

We all found ourselves staring at Svend, as blank and expectant as students in a classroom.

"Being religious might be a valuable adaptive strategy," he lectured, dabbing at his mouth with a linen napkin, "because it lets us minimize the fear of death, and relax. Concentrate on building and fighting. But you see why people become addicted to it. "

"No," said Kate, glaring, "I don't see."

"Oh, come now," murmured her father, ducking his head as he sawed at a tidbit of ham, "we all know that religion has a palliative effect, like scotch, or sex—" and here he shot a sidelong glance at Rose, who looked down at her plate and blushed. "Belief numbs the pain of having evolved an awareness." Svend scanned the table with his bright, dark eyes. Was he not right, was this not obvious?

My mother simply shrugged, sipped from her wineglass, said, "Where I am, death is not. Where death is, I am not." She dismissively flicked crumbs from her slacks. "Why be afraid of death when you will never be conscious of it?"

"Oh, come on, Mum," I protested, "That would work like a charm if you were unexpectedly shot in the back of the head, but what if you fell off a cruise ship, or something, and bobbed around in the water for several days, calling and calling until you drowned?"

"For Heaven's sake, Frances," she said. "Where do you come up with these scenarios?"

"All I'm saying is that the incalculable variable of having time to think, *oh here I am, dying*, tends to foil your equation, Mum. It's not like people have walked around for millions of years singing 'Happy day! I'll never be acquainted with death, not to worry, best just to carry on roasting the mammoth leg and *que serà, serà.'"

"You are such a goof," said David, smiling his infuriatingly patronizing big brother smile.

"I am *not* a goof," I said, and then beamed a further message at him with my eyes: You Idiot Pompous Drunk. "I'm simply *say*ing, David," a.k.a. Idiot Pompous Drunk, "that the human race hasn't just been generation after generation of fiercely analytical, turtlenecked Scots, like Mum."

At this, I dropped my eyes to my plate, and found myself worrying less about my mother's reaction to this insult than the prospect that I had accidentally bolstered Svend's argument, for suddenly I really deeply hated what he was saying.

"We have seen from research," Svend carried on, as if rejuvenated, "that Moses, St. Paul and Mohammed were epileptics. Their brains—which is to say, their neurons—were misfiring. They triumphed over disability by turning their experience into a prerequisite for human advancement."

"You have no idea what you're talking about," Kate hissed, pushing away her dinner plate for emphasis. "Look at what you're saying. You're basically announcing with your work that you know how a television functions, and then concluding that everything we see on TV is coming from within the TV itself. You've figured out the mechanism! Oh look! It's the brain, it's the TV. It's a *thing*. Everything to you is just a thing."

My uncle shrugged, still smiling. "The existence of God is basically irrelevant to what happens in my laboratory. There could be a God, but it has nothing to do with why people see visions. That is all the magnetic field, and I've shown that, in my work."

"Oh," Kate cried, unhinged, "you're being such a pig! Don't you see that? What you're showing, it's like understanding that the reason we cry is because we have tear ducts. Is that why we cry?"

And here Rose made her fateful mistake, inviting the rude impact of hand-fashioned napkin ring to her cheekbone by interceding between father and daughter. "This is just a theory, Kate," she ventured, "it's nothing to . . . to . . ."

WHACK.

"Oh!" my mother said, abruptly standing. "For *Heaven's sake*."

Rose did not run tearily from the room. She merely sat there dabbing at the reddening welt on her cheek with her napkin through the curtain of her hair. But Kate most certainly ran off, howling into the hallway, setting off the Pomeranians, her birthday party in ruins.

I got up to follow her, kissing everyone quick goodbyes, and ushered her into my car. We drove off in stormy silence as she wept beside me and I zoomed around in special Rosedale circles, cornering the same wet lawns beneath a cold rain until Kate finally gave up sobbing long enough to irritably direct me out of the maze.

When I got home, I found my father and my son asleep on the couch, with Curious George lying open between them, and a world of quiet wonder still intact.

"You don't have to do this, Kate."

"Yes, I do," proclaimed my cousin, with a mirthless smile.

We were in her car this time, her cherry-red Honda, paid for by all her work declaring men to be oafs and control freaks, and we were driving out to Mississauga for a rendezvous with Larry. Only, this time it wasn't me that Kate was aiming to inflame, but her father. And it wasn't rocks and blindfolds she was after. Larry, with whom she had kept in touch, was now doing a booming business in the home manufacture of MDMA. Somewhere along the line, as Kate explained it, Larry had decided that the original shamans of the world were correct to have journeyed on drugs. But he didn't favor psychotropics, which he felt required an advanced level of experience. He declared them too powerful for the ritually uninitiated who attended his beginner workshops, particularly after one attendee took peyote and, instead of lying there blindfolded and listening to the beat of Larry's drum, wandered into the closet beneath the stairs and began drawing patterns in the kitty litter. Larry found this sort of behavior unproductive, and decided to experiment with Ecstasy, which proved a great success.

"You can't do this," I repeated to Kate. "You're a lawyer. You cannot spike your father's scotch with Ecstasy. I mean, you know that."

"Frannie," Kate answered exultantly, tossing her head, "if there were a law that forbade my father from stimulating the brains of innocent U. of T. students and tricking them into a near-death experience, then I would agree with you. But if he can do that, and I can't do this, then the law is an ass. Besides," she added, glancing into her rearview and executing a sharp turn onto Sunny Day Crescent, "if you think that Svend would publicly admit to having been on drugs in order to disbar his own daughter, then you don't know him."

"Do you mind if I wait in the car?" I asked.

While Kate went into Larry's house on her dubious mission, I sat in her Honda and pondered the latest O'Sullivan column, which I pulled out of my bag, unfolded, and read on my lap. This week, he had written that conservatives operated on the basis of fact, whereas liberals ran around being sensitive and touchy-feely. "Socialism doesn't work and this is a fact," he had written. "But Liberals can't deal with facts. Facts make them scream like girls. They just want everyone to have a cozy blanket of socialist health care because it's a 'nice' thing to do. Then they panic when they don't have enough money, and pay for their socialism by raising taxes on those of us who work for a living and can afford our own hospital bills."

Oh, good Lord. What a guy that Sherman was. I worked "for a living" too, didn't I, rectifying his lapses in grade-five grammar while he bowled for breast-access, but nobody gave me benefits. Just the other day, Avery had to sell his first-edition volume of Thackery's *Vanity Fair* to pay for two root canals and some bridge work. *Those of us.* What a goof. I had seen this before, this attack on liberals for being "nice," in the newly militaristic post–September 11 age, where niceness was near to ungodliness. The worst insult conservatives could throw at a public figure was this business of being "nice," which secretly meant, a wishy-washy patsy.

All these characterizations—"nice," "flip-flopping," "liberal"—apparently acted as code for unmanly. Although cops and firemen could be nice, they were never publicly labeled "nice." They were manly men who could tell when a murderer had murdered someone, or a house was on fire. I realized this after scrutinizing a sexy picture spread that Hilary showed me of cops and firemen that had been published in *Washington Wives*. Decidedly absent from this pictorial, called "Heros of 9/11," were the foreign-aid workers, medics, journalists and priests who had also been killed. Perhaps their sexy bravery was canceled out by their odious idealism. Whatever the reason, I never saw them included in glossy neo-con hero porn.

At the same time, I might add—rehearsing my tirade in Kate's car, staring absently out the window with my blood pressure rising—over the years, I had met quite a few nice cops and firemen, and "nice" was actually the first thing that sprang to mind about them. They were kind. Earnest. Often distressed by human nature, but astute and experienced about its complexities. And when they *did* see the world in black and white, Mr. Sherman O'Sullivan, for them it wasn't an ennobling picture. According to my mother, who had counseled several "front-line workers," the descent into a black-and-white worldview quickly turned them into drunks.

Gripping the column in my lap, I thought of Bernice in her dinky hospital with its J-Cloth food and its doctors so overworked that they couldn't keep their files straight, and wondered how Sherman could believe that she didn't deserve the bed she slept in. What did she deserve, then? What plea did she need to make for her bed? Sorry we're poor and nice. We try not to be poor. We work on being bloody-minded. We pray every night that God will transform us into self-satisfied goons who wish to run the world, but he doesn't hear our prayers.

I flipped back to the first page, and began erasing the penciled-in punctuation marks I'd made. Then I started over.

"Conservatives are grounded in fact? Because something like government-provided 'socialist' health care is a nice thing to do. Even though it ends up increasing taxes on those of us who 'work' for a living."

That sounded better, I thought.

There was a thump on the roof of the car as Kate hit it with her fist, before swinging open her door and hopping in, tossing back her luxuriant hair.

"A success?" I asked.

"Time to party!"

She practically did a wheelie as she zoomed the car around the cul-de-sac and tore out of the suburbs en route to her weird misadventure.

"Oh shit, I still could use the extra cash," I muttered as Kate roared along the QEW.

"What's that you said, Frannie?" she asked, smiling.

"Pray for me, Kate," I answered. "I'm about to lose a gig."

33

"Do the cells in my body like me?"

Of course, Lester has to ask me this at ten-thirty at night, when I am fed up with his wakefulness, frustrated beyond measure that I am missing *CSI: Miami*, and am instead lying ramrod straight on his lower bunk like an astronaut in a sleep capsule, biding my time until someone in the room loses consciousness.

"They ARE you," I assure him.

"Because *I* like *them*," he offers.

"But, so, what do you think of as 'I'?"

He reflects on that. "Is my soul in my brain, then? Like, my brain tells everything else what to do?"

"You could think of it as your soul being the driver of a car," I allow, trying to correct my voice so that it sounds maternally peaceful rather than howlingly petulant, "which is the body. If the car broke down—remember how our Buick broke down last summer? We didn't die, did we, just the car did. We got out of the car, and got a new one. It's sort of like that."

He considered this. "How big is my soul?"

Aaaargh, relentless.

"Go to sleep," I tell him. "It's far too late for these kinds of questions. You can ask me tomorrow morning at breakfast."

"But I can't go to sleep."

"Why not?"

"I'm afraid I'll get stolen out the window."

"You won't get stolen, that just doesn't happen."

"But that girl, Cecilia, she was stolen out of her window, remember?"

Of course I do. Her sweet little nine-year-old face on every evening newscast, her poster in all of the shop windows, parents pleading for their only child's return. The word spread on the playground, from older kids who could read the headlines, to the younger ones. The germane information that had lodged in his brain was that a sleeping child had been snatched from her very own bed and spirited away through the window. Vanished, never heard from again. Made invisible.

"But that really, really hardly ever *ever* happens," I argued. "It's so very, very rare."

Still, the possibility exists. And how can I reassure him, when I am so very much like him? Was, as a child, and still am. What if there's an Ice Age? It's possible. What if my plane crashes? It might. What if there's a serial killer on the stairs? Well, it's highly unlikely, but it's happened.

Mothers used to be able to defer to a higher authority. "We cannot know what God intends." Say your prayers now, child: "If I should die before I wake, I pray the lord my soul to take."

Without God, we are stranded in a spidery web of statistical probabilities, just windmilling our little legs in the air like stuck flies.

34

"Frannie?"

"Yes?" I held the phone to my ear and tried, at the same time, to reach my coffee mug, to no avail.

"This is Helen."

Oh. Why?

"How are you, Helen?"

"I wanted to remind you," she said crisply, "that you had actually paid for two sessions up front."

"Oh, did I?" Well, never mind, keep the change.

"Fran, if you're willing to follow up with your second session, I want to try another tack. We won't do past-life regression, I assure you. But I do think you could really benefit from hypnotherapy, and different people respond to different methods."

"Okay," I offered, because I could never say no to someone straight to their face. Aaargh. I'm such a wimp.

I told myself maybe I owed her this chance to be vindi-
cated. Once a mother, always a mother, letting people do
their show-and-tell. As soon as I hung up, I began imagining ways to get out of it. My son is sick. My car broke
down. I've come down with Ebola. But as the week progressed I began yearning for some measure of comfort.
Calvin phoned to say that his mother had taken a turn for
the worse, and his defensive emotional tone was so cold
and robotic that I dreamt he was having an affair, carried
on entirely by fax. My brother showed up, unannounced
and weeping, to report that Penny had left him. She'd
met some dink in Baja California with blow-dried hair
and wads of cash, and David's heartbreak blew my
mind. I wanted to hunt her down and riddle her with
bullets from an automatic rifle, my anger on his behalf
was that fierce. Of course I've heard that blood is thicker
than water, but I never would have believed it, if I hadn't
been put to the test.

I missed Calvin, and felt more keenly his sorrow.
And I missed Lester, who was packed off every day to
daycare, with his toys and his snack and his inchoate
sorrow.

In the end I kept the appointment with Helen, driving
up to St. Clair and Yonge that Friday after dropping
Lester off.

"Wait," I said, as I sank into the giant chair. "Helen,
can I clarify something first?"

She nodded, seated at her escritoire, this time in a
natty blue wool suit.

"I take it from our past-life regression thing that you

believe in reincarnation, which would make you . . .
what . . . a Buddhist or a Hindu or something like that?"

She smiled demurely and shook her head. "Not really,
Fran, no. I've just found that this technique is helpful to
many of my clients, and really, what's important is what
they believe, not what I believe."

I studied her, careful. "So you don't believe in reincarnation."

"My spiritual views aren't pertinent, as long as I am
properly trained and very mindful."

How odd. Relativism in service to godliness. I had a
thought: "So then, before I came the first time, you
thought *I* was a Hindu?"

She dipped her head down, embarrassed. "I was
under the mistaken impression that you were a
Buddhist. I apologize."

We gazed at one another in vexed silence.

"The main thing," she finally said, patting her hair and
stretching her shoulders back, "is I appreciate your coming back, and I do have something else that I think will
work very nicely for you. I can see that you're still very
tense, and I do think I can help."

I sighed and threw my head back on the chair. The
truth is, I didn't mind that first bit she did, where she got
me to relax to the point of incontinence. That was alright,
I could do that again. It was either Helen, or an entire
bottle of Jack Daniel's.

"Okay," she said, once she had expertly brought me
through her ritual of relaxation and I was duly tossed flat
on a beach. "Now, I want you to imagine a place. It can

be any place at all, as long as it is your own, secret place. I want you to imagine every part of this place. See it. Are the walls wood, or glass? Are there many bright windows, or is it cozy and dark? What is on the floor? Is it carpeted or smooth? Is there a big feather bed, or just big cushions gathered around a fireplace?"

Gamely, I imagined a place, then several different places, and busily redecorated this way and that until I finally settled on a space of sunlit glass and marble with a white, furry sort of rug on the floor. As an afterthought, I added Brad Pitt, naked.

"Are you in your secret place?" Helen asked. I fluttered my pinkie.

"Gooood. Now, remember that this is your hideaway from the world, a temple of solitude that no one can enter but you."

Reluctantly, I booted out Brad Pitt, but then a few moments later Viggo Mortensen showed up, and what could I do? I had to be polite. He lay down beside me on the furry rug and we began conversing in Elvish.

"Alright, Frannie," Helen said, "good. I want you to focus, for a moment, on your fears about climate change. Think about how you feel as you sit happily and safely in your own private space."

Excuse me, do you mind? I'm lying around naked with *Viggo Mortensen!* Go talk to Al Gore about climate change, if you're so interested in the subject, you bitch!

Oh dear. I wasn't being sufficiently suggestible. Again. I wondered if I should tell her that. On the other hand, I didn't want to confess, for that would break the spell and make me surrender my imaginary sanctum. Me, sunlight, a man whose stringy, unwashed hair is bizarrely alluring, and a furry rug. A corner of heaven. I didn't want the solitude that Helen was coaxing me toward. If it was solace that I sought, then I associated it with something other than being alone. I paired it with whispers and shared pleasure. With feeling fulfilled and serene.

This sensation of loneliness brought a wave of sadness to me as true and deep as anything I had ever felt. Minutes passed in silence. I lay with the feeling for a long time, it seemed, and Helen, to her credit, remained motionless and perfectly quiet.

At last, after one hundred and twenty-five million years, I struggled to sit up.

"You've seen something," she said gently, with a half-smile.

"It's nothing," I told her, blinking, running my hand shakily through my hair. "I mean, it's just that I understood or felt something that I guess was there all along, this powerful sense of being alone." I shrugged. Uncertain. "That's all."

Back out on Yonge Street under the pale, subtly brightening sky of early March, I walked past the windows of Bregman's Deli, where my aunt Mary used to take me with Kate for bagels and cream cheese when my mother had to work on a Saturday. It was early on in Mum's psychotherapy practice, and she couldn't afford to ask anyone to shelve their neuroses till Monday. I remembered carving faces in the cream cheese with my straw. I couldn't eat the bagel until the face was complete, perfected to my satisfaction, and then I would dreamily efface it with my tongue. Kate would make faces in her bagel too, and then stab it with a toothpick. I cannot recall what Aunt Mary was doing, or thinking, on her side of the table, although I realize now that it was around the time she was being abandoned in slow motion by Uncle Svend.

Later, in university, I would sometimes drag myself into Bregman's with a hangover and a man I'd just slept with, and we'd sit in giddy silence, clouded by the secretive sense of our having had sex, sipping coffee and picking at scrambled eggs. And later that same day, I remember calling one of those men from a pay phone, still dreamy like a kid, wanting to know when I'd see him again, and he told me, sheepish, that he couldn't go out—he "had a date"—and I stood there at the pay phone, as sharply and abruptly wounded as if I'd been hit with shrapnel.

So much makes you alone. The men who love you, but don't. The shopkeepers who pretend to be friendly, but aren't. The fathers who negate your desire to believe in them. The doctors who keep secrets they don't care about, while you stay in the dark. The ideologues who make you feel like crap for being human, like the worst sin you could commit in the world is not knowing where you are going, no matter how openhearted your path.

"We will have to choose between two ways of being crazy," the priest Jean Vanier once wrote, "the foolishness of the Gospel, or the nonsense of the values of our world."

35

Monday morning. No quote from Avery today, just a relayed message. "Sherman wants to talk to you." A pencil tapped against his head.

Of course Sherman did. I went down the hall, and hovered at the threshold of his office, braced for my scolding.

"Sherman?" I ventured, when I caught his attention. "Avery said that you'd been looking for me."

He was seated at his polished mahagony desk, staring down at a copy of the *Moral Volcano*, his anger evident in the clenching of his jaw.

"People," he said, without looking up, "are making fun of me for my latest column, Frances. They say it reads as if it were translated from Turkish by Google."

"Oh," I said vaguely, and shrugged.

"I trusted you with my writing, Frances," he continued. "That's why I gave you the last sign-off before it went to print." He locked eyes with me. "I don't mean to pry," he added, his tone turning acid, "but you aren't having a nervous breakdown of some sort, are you? An episode in your life that is making you want to lash out?"

"Oh, look," I answered, as I felt heat flush my cheeks, "it's funny that you should mention not wanting to pry, because I have been feeling the same way. Like, I've been dying to ask you if you have ever been to France, and if that's where you met Gail, or whether you formed your bizarre ideas about Gallic politics after watching *La Cage aux Folles.*"

He leaned back in his leather desk chair and steepled his fingers, regarding me as if a chill had just gone up his spine.

"What do you mean?" he wanted to know, careful.

I stuck out my lower lip and shrugged. "I went to France when I was nineteen, and I had a good time; the crêpes in Brittany were unbelievably delicious."

Somewhat undone by the stupidity of what I'd just said, I soldiered on. "And you know, I found the French could be insufferable, particularly in their disdain for your ability to speak French properly, and also if you dared accuse a waiter of ripping you off in a restaurant, God forbid." I rolled my eyes. "But what confuses me, in what you've been writing, is that I can't say that I ever got the impression that the French wanted to take over the United States by brainwashing liberals." I looked at him. He had no response. So I continued, "And so . . . I've been worrying . . . I don't know if I'm editing you for sense in that sense, because I'm not sure you're actually capable of making sense. In what you say about the French. "

"What is it that goes over your head, precisely?" he inquired.

"I guess what it is, Sherman, is that I can't edit you for sense when the argument you make, sense-wise, is that half of the American population is in the thrall of a bunch of guys in Paris. Or when you argue that poor people in Canada don't deserve to die in hospital beds if they can't afford them. And that abortion is a feminazi tryanny. You pose a challenge for me that transcends figuring out where the commas should go, because—"

"Ah," he interrupted, reaching for his phone as if to dismiss me, "the truth comes out, doesn't it. You cannot betray your cause."

"My cause?" I echoed, and now my ears were ringing like someone had just clanged a pair of cymbals two feet away. "I worry about you saying things like that, Sherman, because it's so paranoid. The truth is, I've never really thought about whether I was a liberal, or a what, until you started throwing cartoon versions of human experience at me." I stopped hovering on the threshold of his office and marched in, energized by my need to get this off my chest.

"You know, I can't even figure out what you mean by 'liberal.' You're actually using the word as if you're referring to 'the Japs' in World War II. It's like . . . enemy rhetoric. Oh, lo, here cometh the foul tribe of Canaan. Who do you mean, Sherman? Your fellow Canadians, all shopping together at Costco and watching *Hockey Night in Canada*? I'd say they're about as dangerous as hobbits at a gardening show. Is that the apocalypse you see coming, Sherman, your fellow Canadians puttering through garden shows and terminating pregnancies and getting cancer and needing beds? Have you visited the Congo lately?"

"Poor little liberal girl," he murmured, avoiding eye contact as I prowled his office.

"What makes you say that?" I persisted. "I agree with certain things, and not others, but they don't break down along clear lines. Oh!" I had a thrill of revelation as I studied his face. "That makes me undecided, or a 'moderate'—right? Too complicated, too wishy-washy in my thinking. So, in your mind, I *am* a liberal, aren't I?"

"Please leave," he urged, assuming an expression of utter contempt and reaching once again for his phone.

"Oh, no," I said, "I'm not finished." Indeed, I was so intent I felt like Columbo in a wrinkled raincoat, unraveling the incriminating truth. Of course, Sherman wasn't remotely listening at this point; he'd just shut down. It was like arguing with an iguana. Unable to reach him with words, I threw my bagel at him. A crescent of toasted pumpernickel glanced off his shoulder, leaving a smear of cream cheese on his fine wool jacket and landing with a soft thud on his desk. Spluttering in surprise, he hung up the phone.

"I'm sorry, Sherman. I wasn't finished. You weren't listening. Hear me out, if you don't mind, or I'll throw another snack." I sat down on a chair by the window and leaned toward him. "Here's what drives me crazy. You and your magazine, you stake out the moral high ground, that's your whole raison d'être, isn't it? With your disapproval of abortion and gay marriage and what you call liberalism? But you're childish. You have no empathy, you just toss around stereotypes. You publish Ann Coulter, for God's sake, who sneers that all the 'pretty women' are Republicans. She shows about as much talent for argument as a child throwing a water balloon out the window. Have you not *noticed*? Or is it all just a game, where you get to show off to each other about who's sauciest and boldest in their snickering? You remind me of the artistocrats before the French Revolution, trading bon mots at soirees while the mobs gathered."

He gave a theatrical sigh. I got up and started heading for the door. But I paused at its threshold and turned back.

"Just ask yourself this one question. Where is your moral high ground? Really, that is what I want to know more than anything else. Is the God who told you to oppose abortion and liberals the same God who bids you to act like a grade-school brat? Can you point it out to me in your sacred texts sometime, where it says 'Lo, you must stomp on French bread and pull hospital beds out from underneath the backsides of the poor?' Where are you getting your convictions from, Sherman? From God? I notice that the Pope opposed the war in Iraq, and so did the Archbishop of Canterbury. Or are you Buddhist?"

"Get out!" he shouted at me, swooping down to clutch my bagel and throw it back at me. I ducked and it shot into the common lounge and smacked against the UN poster.

"Okay," I said, throwing my arms up, "fine."

I was filled with adrenaline and gumption, but it wasn't fine. All I had managed to do was engage in a food fight.

36

"Hey, you," said Kate, popping her head into my office the next day.

"Good Lord," I said, looking up in startlement from my newspaper, "what are you doing here?" My nerves were a bit frayed.

"Court was canceled," she explained with a smile, striding into the room and unwinding her long green scarf. "Gotta minute?"

"Of course I have a minute," I said, gesturing in exasperation at all of the books and galleys and manuscripts piled pell-mell on my desk. "All I have to do is figure out what's a Must Read for spring. Any suggestions? What do women in the middle of divorces want to read?"

"The Riot Act," Kate said.

Avery returned from a visit to the bathroom down the hall. "Oh," he exclaimed. "Hello, Kate." He scratched his neck reflexively and then stuck out his hand as if to shake hers, but almost instantly retrieved it and jammed it into his pants pocket.

"Mr. Dellaire," Kate said, her voice faintly teasing, for she sensed that she made him nervous. "I haven't seen you since that fundraiser for literacy at the Women's Bookstore. How are you, sir?"

"Oh. Tolerably well," Avery replied, nodding his head too much, and smiling with self-conscious pleasure. This was interesting. I'd never seen Avery thrown off by the presence of a girl.

"Don't let me interrupt you," Kate said, gazing at us both.

"No, not at all," Avery rushed to assure her, taking his seat and then standing up again. Kate dragged Goran's chair over to my desk, sat down and fished something out of her coat pocket. It was a packet of Smarties. "Guess who I'm having dinner with tonight?" she inquired mischievously, waving the box at me. I knew what was in it, in addition to the chocolate Svend was fond of.

"Oh no, Kate. No," I protested. "You can't do this. It's nuts."

I was incredulous, for I'd assumed she'd get over the impulse. I took a swipe at the box in her hand but she yanked it away and leapt out of her seat. "Come on, Kate," I persisted. "You're a Quaker, for God's sake. Isn't it against your beliefs to drug men?"

Avery was now talking on the phone, and watching us in bemusement. I lunged again for the Smarties box and this time, I snatched it out of her hand. Without further thought, I stood up and ran, and Kate began to chase me, around and around the office until both of us were giggling hysterically. She cornered me, and I thrust the box at Avery. "There's trouble in there," I yelped through my laughter. "Hide it for me, or she'll feed them to her dad."

Thoroughly flustered, Avery grabbed up the box as Kate ran straight for him. He held it high to his chest and she tried to wrestle it free. Just as she seemed to be reclaiming her prize with a tenacious grip, he broke away and rushed into the corner of our office. He found himself at the opposite end from the door, thus foiling any chance of flushing the box down the toilet in the hall. Kate charged toward him, her scarf sliding off her shoulder and spooling to the floor, the pair of us still laughing our heads off. Avery, caught up in his mission and panicked by her approach, suddenly upended the box into his mouth.

"Oh. Whoa, time out!" Kate announced, halted in her tracks in sheer surprise. "Avery, what are you doing?"

I darted over and eased the box from his grip as he choked slightly, trying to swallow. "No, no, no, bad idea," I said, whisking it away. Kate and I immediately bent our heads together to examine the contents. "How many did you buy?" I asked.

"Four," she said.

"How many are left?"

She shook out the Smarties, and then fished out the Ecstasy tablets and studied them in her palm. "Three."

"Oh, fuck," we said in unison.

"Avery, are you insane?" I asked. "What did you do that for?"

"I wasn't thinking," he answered, beginning to pace in distress. "I just—I formed half a strategy."

"With no exit plan," said Kate.

"Alright," I mused, thinking aloud as I steered Avery over to his desk and made him sit down. "Okay. What time is it? Nine-thirty? How long does the drug last, Kate?" She pushed up her coat sleeve and looked at her watch. "He'll be fine by two-thirty," she guessed.

"Oh, Christ!" moaned Avery. "Are you saying that oversized Smartie I swallowed was a drug?"

"This is not going to be a problem," Kate replied, assuming the crisp tone of someone taking command in a crisis. "It's not a psychedelic, Avery, it's just Ecstasy. If anything happens, and I'm not saying it will, if you can't handle it or you want to lie down or something, we can take you home. Not a problem."

"Oh, for God's sake," I muttered, rubbing my face, "this is so ridiculous." I looked at my cousin. "How do you manage to take my nutty life and make it certifiably insane?" I jabbed a finger at her. "Your penance for this mishap, Kate, is that you have to surrender those other tabs to me. You must forfeit your box of Smarties."

Kate was nothing if not scrupulous in her sense of justice. Still, she hesitated. "Oh, give it up, Kate," I argued. "There's a law somewhere, surely, that prohibits you from getting two unsuspecting people stoned on the very same day." She sighed, gave a dramatic shiver, and placed the Smarties on the windowsill. I plopped down in my chair and took a sip of tepid coffee. "Is Larry reliable with drugs?" I suddenly asked. "Like, how do we know that Avery didn't just swallow a hit of talcum powder cut with speed?"

Kate raised her eyebrow, and made a dignified show of rewinding her scarf. "Larry uses MDMA in his shamanic practice," she said with mild indignation. "In exactly the way it was originally designed and approved for psychiatric use before it got banned. He's *very* careful."

"Okay." I nodded, appeased. Avery was pacing again, trying to shake off the shock of what he'd done to himself at the outset of a busy Tuesday morning. I watched him for a moment, and then glanced at Kate, shaking my head. He had not, as far as I knew, ever experimented with a synthetic drug. I had tried Ecstasy once in New York with my friend Marina in Central Park, an experience that left me so peaceful and grass-stained that when we attempted to cap the afternoon with our customary cocktail at the Algonquin, I got asked for ID. That was the first time it occurred to me that looking old had less to do with being old than with feeling burdened by the dead weight of the world.

"Look, don't worry, Avery," I said. "You're not going to take a spooky trip and think you're seeing spiders. Or anything like that. I'm sure it will be fine. It's more like an opiate than anything."

Kate hastened to agree, and then left, after scribbling down her cell phone and pager numbers and apologizing to Avery. She promised to take him out for roast turkey "deluxe" at Canoe. A date with her would be his consolation prize for a day of being stoned out of his mind.

Fifteen minutes later, Avery still felt normal, so the two of us resumed working at our desks. Maybe the whole incident would go away. At ten-thirty or so I was picking up my phone to call a potential reviewer when Avery remarked from his end of the room, "Well, I can't say I'm familiar with drugs, Frannie, but I do find it interesting that my legs feel really good in my pants."

"That's nice, Avery," I said, and put the phone back down and gazed at him curiously. He placed his hands palm-down on his desk and stretched out his fingers, studying them.

"Really, when you think about it," he reflected, "wood has a remarkably smooth texture. Especially when you flatten your hands against it. It feels very harmonious and welcoming." He seemed to consider that for a moment, and then he had an idea. He slowly lowered his head and laid his cheek on his desk. "It works with your face, too," he announced after a few minutes. "I don't know why I never thought of this before."

"What about when you walk around?" I asked, amused. "How does it feel on your feet?" He stood up and took a few steps. "It's wonderful," he said, marveling. He hopped experimentally. Did a few jumping jacks. Then, abruptly, crouched down and carefully executed a forward roll. He sat up smiling. "Frannie, you should try this. I never realized you could roll over on your head on hard wood. "

"Well, it *is* an intriguing discovery, Avery," I offered cheerfully, "but I was actually just about to make a phone call." He ignored me, intent upon his own small pursuits. For the next little while, I tried to think about the Must Reads for spring and juggle phone calls and e-mail while my associate editor felt objects and provided me with a running commentary on their wonderful intrinsic traits.

A publicist called, wondering if I would include a review of a particular author. "Well, I'm certainly considering it," I said, cupping my hand over the receiver to block her from hearing Avery, who was just then expressing his admiration for the gentleness of paper towels.

Finally I gave up and closed my notebook. "How's it going, Avery?" I asked. He was lying on the floor, bent at the hip with his legs pressed up along the wall.

"It's funny how much you take for granted," he replied. "Here I've been in this office for a good three years, and I don't think I've ever really noticed it before. It has so much to offer. Why haven't we ever thought to have our editorial discussions over at this wall before, I wonder."

I laughed. "I'm quite jealous of you right now," I said. And I was. What a sweet experience to get out of one's tormented head, and instantly achieve what the shamans and hypnotists and yogis so tirelessly aim you toward.

"Why don't you take some of this stuff?" Avery asked. "Kate left it here, didn't she? On the windowsill. I think you have to, Frannie. I need you to understand what I'm saying about the wood. "

I looked at my watch. I didn't have to collect Lester from Tweedle Dee until six. "Okay," I agreed, feeling a surge of daring. "But only if you barricade the door. There's no way I'm dealing with Hilary or Sherman. Or a courier, or something."

"Alright," Avery said gamely. He swung his legs over his head, rose to his feet, and went off to the closet beside Goran's desk. He retrieved a pair of my high-heeled shoes, and placed them carefully in front of the door.

"I don't think so, Avery," I said, chuckling. I followed him over and slid the bolt across. Then I leaned my head against the door and sighed. "I can't do this."

"Why not?" he asked, taking up a position on the windowsill, which he proceeded to proclaim the most comfortable four-inch-wide perch he had ever had the honor of resting upon in his life.

"I can't get stoned, Avery. It would be cheating. I'm in the middle of a whole lot of sobering things. I need to stay in control of myself."

"Ah, Frannie," he mused, tilting his head back as if he were sunbathing, there on the windowsill on a rainy Toronto morning. "Do I look out of control to you? Or do I look relaxed?"

I returned to my desk and sat down, pondering him for a minute. "You look relaxed," I allowed. "You haven't scratched your neck or twisted your arms in at least an hour."

"Weren't you the one, Frannie," he continued, "who theorized to me that the people who insist on absolute explanations and strict standards are the ones who fear losing control?"

"Yes," I answered, "but I'm not talking about a life-view, Avery, I'm talking about not getting stoned today, because I'm responsible for rather a lot at the moment, and it seems ill-advised."

"Ah, Frannie," Avery said again, and then he went on a brief tangent about how the sound *ah* felt really wonderful coming out of his mouth, and he understood why yogis liked to say *om*. "Anyway," he said to himself. "Where was I? Oh. Yes. Ah, Frannie. Here's what I wanted to ask. Has it ever occurred to you that this God you seek eludes you because you're afraid to lose control?"

"Jesus, that took you a long time to spit out." But then I considered what he had said.

"Okay, Avery," I finally answered. "I'm going to do this for you, and for the practice. To rehearse what it's like to open up and let go."

For forty minutes after I chased a tablet of Ecstasy with tepid coffee, I soberly listened to Avery's observations and insights, and was fascinated when he elected to explain his thing about turkey. "It's one of the only things I remember about her," he said. "The roast turkey I helped her prepare for Thanksgiving, the month before she died. I don't know what it was about that, whether it was the goodness of the meal, or the excitement of the occasion or the fact that I did a commendable job cutting up the parsley for the stuffing. But I remember it. And I hunger for it again and again."

BELIEVE ME

Moved beyond words, I went over to hug him, which caused him to remark upon how soft a hug can feel. And then I joined him in this world of being present, and surrendered. The two of us lay side by side on the floor of our office, feeling as flat and still as two body shapes chalked at a crime scene, and for the next few hours talked about the people we loved, and how much we loved them, including Bono of U2 and William Thackeray and the guy at my local Starbucks, and then of the people we forgave, for all of us were nothing if not stumblingly human, and finally of the unheralded gentleness of a hardwood floor, as shared between lifelong friends.

37

Lester and I flew back out to Cape Breton when March blew in like a lion, pelting our Jetsgo airbus with frigid rain. Unperturbed by the weather, my son sipped his ginger ale and inexpertly colored a picture of Spider-man while I reflected on the last time I had seen Bernice living her life with Stan.

It had been early September—the Labor Day before last. We had all gone out together to visit, and one afternoon, Calvin took Lester to the New Waterford playground while I lay on the couch, felled by a stunning headache, with Stan sitting nearby on his easy chair and watching a ball game.

"Oh . . . my . . . God!"

We both heard her tremulous protest waft out of the kitchen. But Stan didn't rise from his chair, just registered her voice with a mild flinching uplift of his hand, which clutched the remote.

"Stan?"

She had come into the archway that separated sitting room from dining room, kneading the gnarled backside of her hand. Her pink terrycloth bathrobe was stained in purple blotches from her pie-making.

"Stan, the microwave's broke! There's air blowing out of it, look." She gestured backward. "I'm cooking your bacon and I can feel this little wind coming out. Oh my God. It must be radiation escaping."

"It's the way those things work, Bernice," Stan said irritably, but he got up anyway, shuffled to the kitchen in his corduroy slippers and had a look.

"Can you feel it?" she asked.

"Sure I can."

Bernice sank into a kitchen chair, plump feet crossed at the ankles, staring wanly at the floor. "Well, that's not the way it's supposed to work—why would it work that way, eh Stan? Makes no sense! Shirley says there's a sale at the mall, got herself a toaster oven for half-off yesterday. I think you should get another one, get a replacement."

"What am I supposed to do with the bacon?" he asked, peering dubiously into the gleaming white box.

"I'll just make some fresh in a pan." She raised herself, looking formless in her billowy robe. He'd make the bacon, himself, he told me later, "don't like the way she fries it, too greasy, but she won't let me. She needs to keep in motion, she says. What the hell for? I ask her." He shook his head in bemusement. "What's she cooked already today, Fran? Eh? Two loaves of bread, strawberry pie, it ain't even mid-morning."

He retired to the bathroom with the *National Enquirer.* The phone rang, searing my temples, and Bernice went to answer it.

"Stanley?" she called, after a moment's conversation.

"Well, hold on there," he yelled back, "I'm in the john, not running nowhere with my pants down."

"Dr. Richardson's on the phone, I won't talk to him," she cried.

Stan came hopping out, tucking his plaid shirt into worn brown pants. "Come on, Bernice, you're waving the phone like a damn live grenade."

It was true, I noticed from my vantage point pretending to sleep on the couch. She practically threw it at him before plopping down on a dining-room chair with her eyes squeezed shut. He held the receiver to his good ear and gazed out the window at the KFC.

"How you doin', Johnny?" He listened for a beat, then: "I'm not getting down to the hall much this year, no. I miss the games, sure I do, but it's hard gettin' out with her so nervous, you know."

Whatever Richardson told him then, I knew Bernice was expecting some blood test results, for something or other. High-blood pressure, as I recall.

"Sure, I do," said Stan. "Oh, I'll try to bring her in, sure." He sounded noncommittal. Last time they went up to the Regional, he told me, Bernice clung to the doctor's doorway like a cat about to have a bath. Occurred to him he should have brought her in a carrying cage,

243

she was that uncooperative. Now he glanced down at his wife, at the tight little curls on her head interspersed with patches of shell-pink skin. I wondered what he was thinking, that she had straight hair once, straight and thick and lovely. That he missed the woman who had that hair.

"Hand me that pen there, will you, Bernice?" he asked.

She stared up at him, miserable, her mouth such a trembling upside-down crescent she was almost cartoonish. I felt a heated anger within me somewhere, fleeting as a spark. I hated it that you could see right through her sometimes, like you could a little kid.

After jotting something down, Stan hung up, and Bernice made herself busy again, as if the world would end if she didn't keep moving. She started poking around in the blond-brown cupboards she'd had Stan install that summer, finally pulling out a jar of flour. She whirled around, lips moving silently, heading for the fridge to see if there were any eggs left. "I got eggs," I heard her mutter, "I got oil, I got water, maybe I should put something else, I could put in some coconut maybe, like Shirley was sayin', tasted real good in brownies." She sank to her knees and started rifling through odds and ends in the side panel, maraschino cherries and such.

"Stan? Can you get down to Sobey's for bananas and some coconut, the shredded kind, comes in a little bag in the spice section, then go over to Mayflower and see about the microwave sale Shirley was telling about. And get one of them filters too, for the humidifier."

He obeyed without remark, reaching for his raincoat, patting his back pocket for his wallet. He lifted his tweed hat off the stand and slipped away.

"Stanley?" I heard the soft *whuff* of the door pulling shut against the wind.

Bernice knelt before her meat crisper and frantically imagined supper: meat pie or roast—Stan said he was tired of fish cakes. "What about you, Nancy? Does Lester like meat? I could do up a ham."

"Whatever's easiest for you," I called from the couch, as if ease had anything to do with it. I switched off the TV. Now I could hear Stan's favorite country music station playing on the radio in the kitchen, the little transistor spitting static and twang from the counter beside their new stove. A commercial announced a sale on boxsprings at Sleep Country, and then the news came on. "Hurricane Don continues to bear down on North Carolina today, with forecasters predicting landfall somewhere between Charlotte and Wilmington late this afternoon." This news provoked wide-eyed attention from Bernice. "The storm is expected to reach the Maritimes possibly as early as tomorrow," continued the radio man, "bringing gusting wind and heavy rain to coastal areas."

"Oh . . . my . . . God!"

The ham she'd pulled out of the fridge rolled heavily out of her lap as she heaved and floundered on the floor, scrabbling along the linoleum to hoist herself up by Stan's breakfast chair. "It's gonna flood my basement and ruin the dryer."

I couldn't follow her logic, but her muttering became a mantra—"the dryer oh my God"—as she headed for the basement door. I got up, my head pounding, and followed her to make sure she was okay. Down in the basement, she was caught up wildly in frantic, cockamamie schemes to keep things dry, yanking plugs out of the cold wall, throwing towels around, dragging at bags of grass seed as if she could sandbank the cellar, muttering her mantra, getting dizzy until finally she careened against the bottom steps and ran aground, perspiring.

"Bernice?" I ventured, hovering beside her with a towel in my hand in case she wanted me to mop her forehead, which was the least of her concerns.

She began crying, her shoulders rising and falling in shudders. "Hurricane's gonna ruin my dryer," she sobbed.

"What hurricane?" asked Calvin, suddenly behind me, halfway down the stairs. "There isn't going to be a hurricane, Mum."

"Hurricane Don!" she bellowed at him over her shoulder, righteous and grieving. "It's comin' up the coast."

"What are you talking about?" he retorted, sounding like his father. "It won't be anything to worry about by the time it gets up here. Come on, Mum, come on up. I'll make you a cup of tea." He descended the stairs to take her hand.

Later that afternoon, with Stan back and on his knees playing with Lester, Bernice had another hurricane-related revelation.

"Oh my God, the patio furniture! It'll blow around and break the windows!"

She pushed past me, wild-eyed, and headed outside, where the sea wind batted at her dressing gown and whipped her white curls. She grabbed up her plastic chairs and waved them around like a lunatic lion tamer fending off ghosts in the salt air. The pinwheels she'd planted in her marigolds spun their wings as fast as hummingbirds, backward and forward as the gusts switched directions. Her chimes kicked and danced, her butterfly feeder bounced, the lantern held by her little black sambo swayed madly, and she seemed to understand all this as Don's approach, his menacing howl coming up the coast from Halifax.

"Bernice!" called Stan, holding open the kitchen door, with Calvin right behind him. Stan stepped outside and reached for her chairs, easing them from her grasp and storing one atop the other before carrying them across the lawn to the shed, a lock of gray hair on his forehead held aloft like a cowlick by the wind. Wordlessly, he and Calvin carted all the furniture to safety: four chairs, a table with an umbrella sticking out of it which Calvin had to cartwheel over the grass, a little side table, waterproof cushions. Then they brought in the new microwave, and boxed up the jams Bernice had made so that Stan could drive them over to the soup kitchen.

Evening came, and with it the remnants of Hurricane Don, an intemperate but not particularly ferocious squall. Bernice was in the kitchen surrounded by pans and cookbooks and a dusty cloud of flour. Her panic swelled and receded with the sound of her chimes in the yard, but she could clearly calm herself with cooking: the ham needed glazing; the potatoes scalloped just so; boiled parsnips, that would be good; and a pan of coconut brownies. She wouldn't let me help her, kept shooing me away, "Oh no, dear, no, no," stirring and slicing till her fingers ached.

Stan and Calvin, chuckling at *America's Funniest Home Videos*, didn't hear the surprised, protesting groan as pain grabbed her around the middle and she, in turn, grabbed for her chair. Stan ambled in on a commercial break and found her bent over, clutching a chocolatey spoon.

"Oh, Bernice," he murmured as I stood by, useless and alarmed. He leaned toward her and gently removed the spoon, carried it like treasure to the sink.

"Don't you dare call Dr. Richardson," she whispered into her lap.

"Alright, Bernice, alright." He dropped the spoon into dishwater with a hesitant, trembling hand. The wind fell quiet. On the roof, now, a steadying drumbeat of rain.

Maybe he died before she did because he had to. She wouldn't let go, wouldn't stop, until he was gone.

We switched planes in Halifax, and took the "puddle jumper" up to Sydney, a plane that vibrated and buzzed like a giant bumblebee, and I tried to get a grip on my fear as Lester trustingly lay his head on my shoulder. We dropped five hundred feet in a downdraft, and I clutched discreetly at my forehead, holding Lester's hand as lightly as I could while I prayed. "Lord, in Your grace give me strength." It was a new prayer for me. I used to scrunch up my eyes on these flights and plaintively call out for rescue. But God wasn't in the business of protecting people from their own inventions. Somewhere along in this journey, I had realized that rescue wasn't God's job.

38

"How are you, Barbara?" I asked the head nurse as Lester and I stepped out of the elevator and collided with a gaggle of pink and purple balloons.

"Oh, not too bad, Frannie!" She smiled, shifting her balloons to the other hand. "Not too bad. It's nice to see ya. Celia got out a couple weeks back, asked me to send her love to Lester." She bent over to tweak his nose. He ducked behind me and she chuckled.

"Oh," I said with genuine pleasure, imagining Celia and Jim out for a celebratory dinner at the Cranberry Nook, "that's great! I'm glad to hear about Celia. How are Julia and Aileen?"

"Julia sleeps a lot. Real quiet. You know. Aileen went home a while back, too, up to her daughter's place in Glace Bay." Barbara tugged at the tie that held her clutch of balloons, and freed a pink one for Lester. "I took her

251

some Easter chocolates last week, they were on sale at Sobey's." She looked down at my son and handed him the balloon, which he accepted with the same surprised reverence with which I might greet a stranger handing me a thousand dollars. "Aa'll excited about the Easter Bunny I'll bet?" He nodded, solemn.

"How is Bernice, Barbara?"

"Oh, not too good, hon." She glanced down at Lester, smoothed out her uniform and chose to say nothing further about Bernice's appetite, or lack thereof. "You go on and see her, hon, Calvin's there now."

I can't say, in that moment, that I had an overwhelming desire to walk down the familiar white-walled corridor, festooned though it was now with yellow chicks and fake green grass in early anticipation of Easter. It tore through me again—rent me straight through the center—that I brought Lester with me this time. Was it careless to expose him to Bernice in her slow transformation? Would it threaten his delicately conceived cosmology, in which humans evolved into angels? This was not, I had gathered from my last call with Calvin, a simple matter of a caterpillar turning into a butterfly. There was the benign cocoon stage to consider, which in this instance took the form of a woman swollen to the point of disfigurement, whose breath rattled.

We came to the doorway of Room 10, to which Bernice had been assigned when it became clear to the nurses that she was deteriorating swiftly. The Regional had a palliative ward, but they only used it for patients who accepted that they were dying. For women like Bernice, they had private rooms on workaday wards for the family to conduct their vigils.

Calvin sat beside his mother as quiet as a schoolboy, with his hands on his knees, his expression hovering somewhere indefinable between stoic and forlorn. He had surrounded Bernice with trinkets from her house. There was the chuckwagon that I'd hidden away from Lester, and the small plastic replica of St. Anne de Beaupré that he'd plugged into the wall as a nightlight. A bingo trophy she had won, some samples of her Knit Wit, a couple of doilies that Calvin had laid out on her metal bed table, smoothed carefully beneath a paper cup of ice water and a bottle of pills.

On the wall above her sleeping head, Calvin had taped up some photographs. Lester at Halloween, costumed rather unconvincingly as a squid. Shirley and her husband at the picnic table in Bernice's garden, sipping rye and Cokes in the pale yellow sunshine of a Cape Breton summer. Stan, from about twenty years ago, maybe, on the cold, rocky North Atlantic beach, shoulders hunched, a cockeyed grin, body lilting to one side with his hand on his jutting hip—his "hoodlum" stance, Bernice called it. And a striking picture of Bernice herself, which must have dated from the late '40s. She was leaning on the rail of a ship with her blond hair blowing carefree around a happy and lovely heart-shaped face. She wore a swish skirt and suit, *très* Princess Grace, and high heels that accentuated the slender curve of her calves. That was the woman whose fur coat I had found in the basement, in amidst the

Christmas knickknacks. I'd been wondering to whom that coat had belonged.

"Daddy!" cried Lester, running to greet his father, who was startled out of distant thoughts by his son's bright voice.

"Small young man!" replied Calvin, grinning in pleasure and reaching out his arms.

I hung back, leaning my head against the door frame, still captivated by what I saw. By the meaning Calvin had been trying to construct of his mother's life, through an assembly of all her small treasures.

"Hey, sweetie," I said as I broke my stillness and walked into the room. He stood, and hugged me, and told me everything and nothing in the clinging strength of his embrace.

39

"Why don't you take Les for dinner at the KFC," I suggested as I set down my suitcase, loosened my coat, and
noticed Lester staring at his granny. "I'll stay here with
her. See if she needs anything."

"Aunt Shirley might come by," he warned, taking
Lester's hand. "She and Mum are still in cahoots over
Mum not dying, and Shirley's looking into a senior's
apartment she wants Mum to rent."

"Okay," I said, giving him a puzzled look. "I thought
they were in the *opposite* of cahoots. Wasn't Shirley refusing to speak to Bernice the last time we talked about it?"

Calvin shrugged and tugged Lester toward the corridor. "It seesaws," he said, grimly, and then to his son,
"Come on, small young man, we are going out to dine."

I almost wailed "Don't go!" I wanted to see more of
Calvin, I hungered for him. I hated, in that moment, that

we had to orchestrate this now in the best interests of our child. Parenthood forced us worlds away when we needed to cling, and yet that was that. Bereft, I hung up my coat beside Bernice's terry bathrobe, and then looked around the room as if I could find something immediate and pressing to do. But there was nothing. A fan whirred quietly in the corner. The nurses, calling back and forth to one another in the hallway, sounded distant. Everything was clean and orderly. Bernice slumbered on in the bed. I sat down and stared for a long time at the pictures on the wall.

I wasn't prepared for the conversation I had with Bernice when she finally aroused from her doze.

"Hand me the blueberries, will you dear, they're in my change purse," she said.

"I beg your pardon?" Her tone was so cheerful and resolute that it felt as if we'd been shopping together at the mall.

"My blueberries, for Heaven's sake," she repeated, impatient.

I might have seen this request as delirious, but with Bernice it hovered within the realm of the possible, given her recent tendency to hide pills in her sneakers, so I checked her small embroidered change purse, which contained nothing but coins. I relayed the unfortunate news.

"Well, where *are* they?" she demanded. "I won't have enough for the pie."

"I'm sorry, Bernice, I don't know where they are," I said, smiling helplessly and wondering why I had to imagine conversations with past-life people and power animals, yet this was the one that was real.

She stared up at the ceiling and sighed. "No one knows *nothin'*."

I couldn't begin to think of a reply. We lapsed into silence and she fell back to sleep.

An hour later: "Oh, good Lord in Heaven," she cried suddenly, scrabbling for my hand, "who let the *geese* in here?"

"What geese?" I asked, startled.

"What do you *mean*, what geese?" she retorted, looking pointedly at the end of her bed. "They're waddlin' all over my kitchen! Go get me my whisk."

"Your whisk?"

"Go on!" She pushed at me, conveying such authoritative urgency that I actually stood up and started looking around for something that might resemble a whisk. "Geese don't like to be whisked," Bernice explained, "it'll scare 'em off my doilies."

At that, I did a double take, and leaned over to stroke her cheek. "Bernice," I said, gently, "there aren't any geese in here. Your doilies are fine."

"OF COURSE there's no geese," she answered, like I was insane, "what are you on about? Why would there be geese?"

"Never mind," I said, and sat back in my chair.

And on it went like this, until toward midnight, she sat up as lucid as Einstein and said, "Nancy, you're back. Thank the Lord you're here, dear, I need to go the washroom. Those nurses, you know they're no good a'taaal.'"

BELIEVE ME

Never in my whole life have I been so relieved and elated by someone's need to go to the washroom. To suddenly be presented with this gift of her coherence, it was thrilling, as if, having reached a straining hand to someone who was falling from a bridge, my grip loosening, their fingers sliding, they came back at the last second with a solid, affirming grasp. Hurrah Bernice! No geese, no purse fruit, just this straightforward need to get up and pee in the bathroom and not in the bed.

I leapt to my feet and assisted her, first to a sitting position, then to slide her pale, heavy legs over and out. She hung heavily on me as we shuffled the ten long feet to the glaringly white bathroom, but it felt like running an Olympic marathon replete with cheering and laurels, for she was wholly herself, complaining the entire way.

"Look at me, I'm a fright," she grumbled, "all swollen up from asthma, feet don't fit my slippers. Oh, they're terrible to me here, Nancy, just terrible. Don't let me buy new slippers. Won't let me out. They've got me locked up like a criminal. Can't get out to the mall."

I lowered her gently onto the toilet, and when she'd finished her business, I handed her some toilet paper.

"Oh, you're a love, Nancy, I'm so sorry you have to see me like this. Can't even wipe myself."

"I've been there." I assured her, "I sprained both my hands, once. Let me tell you, the surprising things you cannot do when you have no hands. Someone else has to pull your underpants up over your bum."

"Stan married me for my bum," she pointed out, as she rearranged her scant hospital gown. Then she waved her hand at me, as if I were a skeptic. "Oh, yes he did, I had quite the bum."

We shuffled back to the bed, arm in arm. "Stan may have admired your bum, but he loved you for your love, you know, for the spark of you."

"Oh, go on," she said, and I had heard her say it just that way to Stan himself, pleased as punch, trying to conceal her smile, "Oh, go on, Stan, you're full of old rope."

"No, he did," I insisted, acting on intuition. "I can tell, the way he loved to tease you, the way he loved your hams, like you were nourishing his soul."

"Oh, he's an old goat, is what he is. A rascal." Present tense.

She settled back into bed and explained how Stan's mother—who had been widowed young by the coal mine and grew deranged in her bitter poverty—had regularly fed her three sons offal thrown out by the New Waterford butcher, picking up discarded "roasts" that she simmered first with vinegar to tease out the maggots.

"Can you just imagine," Bernice concluded.

I shivered. Decent food wasn't just an offering of love, for Stan; it was a loving spoonful of civilization.

"You know, Bernice," I ventured, scrambling around in my purse for a pen and a passable bit of blank paper, which ultimately took the form of an inverted bookstore receipt, "if you're not too tired, I would love it if you could give me the recipe for your Cape Breton meat pie. I've tried to make it at home, but I can't get it right, it never tastes as wonderful as what you make." This was no lie. Bernice and Shirley somehow produced this meat pie—I'd had it every time I was in New Waterford—that I understood to involve shredded beef and pork, but I couldn't replicate its succulent, simple flavor.

She took me through its preparation, step by step, advising me on what cut of meat to buy and what pot worked best for a slow simmer, as confident and content as I had ever seen her.

"Stan married me for my pie," she confided, when I'd finally written everything down, having started on a bookstore receipt, progressed to the inside envelope of my plane ticket and ended on a doily.

"And your bum," I reminded her.

"Oh, go on." She waved her hand in that signature gesture of hers, as if swatting me away.

"You'll see him soon," I said, studying her face. "You know that."

She nodded. For once, she wasn't afraid. "In Heaven," she murmured, shifting over to her side and surrendering to sleep.

"Yes," I said, pulling the thin blanket up over her shoulder. "In Heaven."

40

Early morning. Orderlies preparing to wheel around their trolleys full of toast. I woke up with such a crick in my neck that I felt like I'd swallowed a hanger. No sign yet of Calvin, who was doubtless waiting for Lester to wake up and have his breakfast. I stretched, lolled my head, and had just began wondering if it would be fair of me to split when Shirley rounded the corner. She caught sight of me and jumped like a spooked cat.

"Oh my Lord," she stammered, "you gave me such a fright. I wasn't expecting anyone to be here."

"I'm sorry," I said, stifling a huge yawn, "I was actually just going to leave."

Shirley's corkscrew perm was bedraggled by rain, her pink-tinted spectacles misted over. She tugged at the buttons of her silvery-gray polar parka, which looked just exactly like a sleeping bag. "Well, I hope Bernice didn't give you too much trouble," she ventured, eyeing me dubiously. The last time Shirley had seen me, I was having a panic attack in a bingo hall. She probably didn't think I was up to much. "Bernice can be a handful."

"She was fine," I answered, rubbing my eyes.

"Well, she will be," said Shirley, putting down a tray of Tim Hortons coffees. "Just get this cancer under control with that new drug the doctor's saying about, and I've found her a beautiful apartment over near Sobey's. It's assisted living, you know, so she'll have her own space, own kitchen and all that, but there's nurses in the building."

"Okay," I said, polite.

It reminded me of Kate, what Shirley was doing. Trying to impose her own version of the truth. I couldn't argue her out of it. I left Bernice with her sister and walked out of the hospital. Began shuffling, exhausted, down King Street, splashing in puddles and sniffing the salt air carried inland from the Atlantic.

"Well, hello," said a voice behind me on the sidewalk. "Our young stranger is back in town." It was Father McPhee in a navy-blue pea coat, his hands thrust into his pockets as he strode to catch up with me.

"Oh, hi," I said, unduly pleased to see him. "How are you?"

"Very well, thank you," he replied. We stood smiling at one another on the sidewalk, beside a fire hydrant painted as Papa Smurf. "And you, Frannie? I'm guessing you spent the night at the hospital. Can't get much sleep there."

"No," I agreed. "But it was good. Bernice told me how to make her meat pie. She gave me the recipe."

He grinned. "Now, isn't that something to be treasured." He gazed at me for a moment. "I knew you'd find a way, Frannie. Have you prayed for her, as well?"

I nodded as I ducked my head. I had. I did pray. But there wasn't a simple answer to the assumption behind his question, that I knew there was a God who was listening.

"Why are you out this early?" I asked him, evading the subject.

"Oh, I tend to be on call." He shrugged as he glanced toward the ocean. "I wander out as the occasion requires." He looked back at me and broke out once more into his characteristic grin. "It's good to have Calvin out here, you know. Nice to learn more about Bernice's family. I've actually had a chance to talk to him once or twice." He winked at me. "Says you've been on a bit of a quest this winter. He says listening to you has helped him to think about his dad."

"He said that?" I asked, amazed.

"Sure. Oh, he loves you a lot, Frannie. You remember that in the coming days, when he needs you to be there. He won't know how to ask."

"Okay, I will," I answered, and waved warmly as the priest walked away.

I covered the final block to the house as the sun rose, reflecting on why I'd shied away when he'd asked me about prayer. I still had a journey ahead of me, if I was going to find my way to God.

But it was fair to say this much: I had come a long distance since Jesus was born in December. Ahead of me on King Street, I saw Lester and Calvin coming out of the house and heading in my direction. I waited for Lester to notice me, for him to light up with that wondrous excitement that your small children feel when they see you. Then my anxiety about the days ahead rushed in again, as chilling as the North Atlantic tide.

"Oh, Les," I wanted to say as he ran toward me, clumsy and heedless in his puffy snowsuit, "please forgive me for the days you're about to go through." But I do have a gift, I thought. A direction my son, himself, led me to. A way of talking about faith, a way of caring for the dying. A way of holding steadfast in the world.

PATRICIA PEARSON is a wife, a mother and an award-winning writer. She has won two National Magazine Awards, a National Author's Award and the Arthur Ellis Award for best true crime book for *When She Was Bad*. Her first novel about the life of Frannie Mackenzie, *Playing House*, was nominated for the Stephen Leacock Memorial Medal for Humour. She lives in Toronto with her husband and two children.